Daisy Morrow, Super-sleuth!

The Fourth One:

Pirates of Great Yarmouth
Curse of the Crimson Heart

R T GREEN

R TWO RAVEN

Other books…

Daisy Morrow, Super-sleuth:

The first one: The Root of All Evil
The second one: The Strange Case of the Exploding Dolly-trolley
The third One: A Very Unexpected African Adventure
The fifth one: The Terrifying Tale of the Homesick Scarecrow
The sixth one – Call of Duty: The Wiltingham Enigma

The Pale Moon / Red Mist Series –

Pale Moon: Rising
Pale Moon: Phoenix
Pale Moon: Fearless
Pale Moon: Phantom
Pale Moon: Feral
Pale Moon: Phenomenal
Pale Moon: The Box Set – books 1-3

Red Mist –

Red Mist: Falling
Red Mist: Phoenix
Red Mist: Fearless
Red Mist: Phantom
Red Mist: Feral
Red Mist: Phenomenal
Red Mist The Box Set – books 1-3
Red Mist Box Set 2 – books 4 - 6

The Raven Series –

Raven: No Angel!
Raven: Unstoppable
Raven: Black Rose
Raven: The Combo – books 1-3

The Starstruck Series -

Starstruck: Somewhere to call Home
Starstruck: The Prequel
(Time to say Goodbye)
Starstruck: The Disappearance of Becca
Starstruck: The Rock
Starstruck: Ghosts, Ghouls and Evil Spirits
Starstruck: The Combo – books 1-3

Little Cloud
Timeless
Ballistic
Cry of an Angel
The Hand of Time
Wisp
The Standalones

Contents

5

COME AND JOIN US!

We'd love you to become a VIP Reader.

Our intro library is the most generous in publishing!
Join our mail list and grab it all for free.
We really do appreciate every single one of you,
so there's always a freebie or two coming along,
news and updates, advance reads of new releases...

Head here to get started...
rtgreen.net

Introduction

This is the fourth book in the hit Daisy Morrow series. As you might have seen from the first three, our R.E.D. heroine is nothing like you might expect; she's funny, feisty, and has a tendency to get herself in sticky situations. And she definitely has a wicked side!

Before she retired, Daisy had a job very few people ever have, and although in the last few years she's done her best to leave her legacy behind, somehow it manages to keep lurking in the shadows... in more ways than one!

Those of you who know my work will be aware that with the RTG brand, the unexpected is always around the next corner. Daisy is no exception... and very likely has even more corners.

This time Daisy, Aidan and Celia are taking a weekend off, to go on a very special cruise. They're soon to find out just how special it is!

Daisy had her suspicions even before they set sail, but even she had to admit they were perhaps just fantasy, and the weekend away was too tempting to refuse.

But gut feelings are gut feelings...

We hope Daisy will make you smile, and maybe even gasp in surprise and shake your head a little. If she does, that will make us happy people!

Please let us know what you think, either by email, or ideally by writing a review. Every comment is gratefully received... and is listened to!

Enjoy,
Richard and the RTG crew

A SCALE MODEL OF THE BLACK PEARL

How the Third one ended...

Love is a Many Splendored Thing

The British army cargo aircraft wasn't as comfortable as the Emirates flight that had flown them to Uganda just over a week previously. But the crew had been briefed about their secret return cargo, and had rigged up some makeshift seats in the empty hold.

The vast space which held nothing more than a few boxes of bits that were being returned to the UK, and four humans who were hitching a lift, felt cavernous. But it didn't matter. They were going home with one extra passenger, and that meant everything.

Celia was asleep. As soon as the rescue helicopter had reached Laikipia air base, two female Kenyan nurses had whipped her away, given her several doses of benzodiazepines, together with something to help her sleep, which had worked better than anyone expected. As the morning light came, and still three parts asleep, she'd been helped onto the British transport aircraft, and then, assisted by the comforting drone of the engines, had fallen fast asleep even before they'd reached the North Africa coastline.

Daisy, sitting next to her, gazed at her with eyes full of a mother's love. 'Look at her, dear. She looks so thin.'

'She was always thin,' smiled Aidan, sitting on the other side of Celia. 'But yes, she needs a little of my gourmet cooking therapy.'

'You might have to cook rather a lot, Dip.'

15

'Whatever it takes, Flower. I know there's a long road ahead of us, but there's a light at the end of our tunnel now. With a lot of love and TLC, we'll all get there.'

Sarah nodded her head. 'You two are up to it. Awesome respect to you both. You never gave up... and we might have left our mark on Uganda, but it was worth every minute.'

Daisy narrowed her eyes. 'I wonder what happened to the general.'

'He's most likely in Rwanda or somewhere now, living in a mud hut, unable to sleep for fear someone's going to kill him,' said Aidan.

'I hope someone does,' Sarah growled.

Daisy found a cheeky grin. 'So what do you think of Uganda, Sarah dear?'

She shook her head, but smiled at the same time. 'Well, I could say it was so exciting, but maybe it was the kind of excitement I could do without.'

— — —

One week later, Anton Kowalski watched as the heavy door swung open, and a small, white-haired man appeared, shielding his eyes from the late-morning Ugandan sun. He looked back momentarily as the door thudded shut behind him, and then cast his eyes to the Volkswagen sitting fifty yards away.

Anton climbed out, waved to him. *'Joseph!'*

The elderly man walked slowly over. 'Mr. Kowalski? They said you would be here to pick me up. But why?'

He grinned. 'It's Anton, please. Let's just say I wanted to put the lid of closure on things, in the best possible way.'

16

'They tell me you had much to do with my release. I wish to thank you. But I had thought Florence would want to be here to collect me.'

'That's my fault. I persuaded her to let me do it. She's waiting for you, so get your butt in the passenger seat, and let's not keep her waiting any longer.'

Anton pulled into the brick-weave driveway of Michael's home in Ntinda. Florence's Toyota was parked up against the garage door. Joseph let out a deep, emotional sigh.

'My son had a nice house. I feel so unhappy he is not here to enjoy what he created, all because of me.'

'I can't disagree, it is indeed tragic. But what you have to remember Joseph, is that you fell foul of an evil man, and you knew if you didn't keep your mouth shut, both you and that little lady waiting for you wouldn't be here now.'

'I know, Anton. But it is still not easy to live with.'

'But you are living, Joseph. And you owe it to your son's memory that you enjoy the rest of your time to the full. That's what he wanted, after all.'

Joseph nodded. 'I cannot argue with that.'

'You ready for this?'

He sucked in a deep breath. 'Yes, I think so.'

They walked to the front door, and Anton knocked loudly. No one answered, so he knocked again. There was still no answer, but then someone appeared around the side of the house. Florence walked slowly up the steps to the porch, never taking her eyes off Joseph. Her face showed no emotion, masking the hundred emotions trying to burst out of her.

She came to a stop, four feet from her husband.

'Joseph.'

'Florence.'

'You silly, stubborn man.'

'I had to protec…'

He didn't get any further. As the tears rolled down her cheeks she fell into him, and he wrapped shaking arms around her, held her in a tight embrace they'd not been able to enjoy for fifty-six years.

Anton stepped back a little, feeling like his job was done, and not willing to intrude on their private reunion he had no further part in. Lost in their embrace, neither said a word. 'Be happy, you two,' he said quietly, and turned to leave.

Florence finally broke away from her husband, called out to him. 'Please, Mr. Kowalski, don't go. I have prepared a little food, on the terrace. A celebration. Please join us.'

'It is kind of you, Florence, but I will say no. Today is for you two, not for someone who is a total stranger.'

Florence shook her head, smiled to him. 'I think you are not a total stranger. At least take tea, and do not insult my hospitality.'

It was said with no malice, but Anton knew he actually would insult them if he did not stay a little longer. He nodded, followed them as they walked hand in hand to the terrace, where what looked like a feast had been laid out on a table under a big green parasol.

Florence disappeared into the house, and reappeared three minutes later with a tray of milky teas. She handed one to Anton. He sipped it thoughtfully, and then spoke to his hostess.

'I gotta say, Florence, General Oyite met his end in a very ironic way… some would say a fitting one.'

She wouldn't look at him. 'I would include myself in those people, Anton.'

He chuckled. 'Guess we'll never know who threw that grenade into the command hut at Entebbe barracks artillery range, hey?'

'I suppose we never will.'

'Yeah, and whoever it was kinda knew the authorities wouldn't spend too much time trying to discover who it was.'

'As you say, it was indeed an ironic way for him to lose his life.'

Anton bid them farewell, and told them he would do all he could to make sure Joseph received compensation for the extra years he'd spent incarcerated for the crime that never really was.

Joseph shook his hand, Florence gave him a hug, and he left them to their private and heartwarming celebration.

As he drove away, a smile broke across his bushy face. It had been a good day, and a fitting lid had been welded forever onto a pot that stank worse than a soldier's boots.

Daisy and her crew had inadvertently shaken a few leaves off branches, and exposed the bare wood of a very old tree. The authorities were no doubt relieved they were safely back in England, and unlikely to visit Uganda again.

But he couldn't help a wave of sadness wafting through him. Doing his thing with an old friend had brought a strange kind of forgotten excitement, one he never thought he would experience again. He would miss the thrill, and miss every one of them, even though their visit had left him without a weekend home!

But none of that could dampen the smile on his face. Despite it all, he couldn't stop one thought running riot through his head.

In so many different ways, love was indeed a many splendored thing.

And now the Fourth One

Pirates of Great Yarmouth:
Curse of the Crimson Heart

Honour Among Thieves

The one-inch diameter diamond drill-bit began to penetrate the thick steel door, the skilful guy wielding the heavy machine knowing exactly where to make the hole.

The other two men watched as it slowly began to sink into the plating. It would be a good ten minutes until it pierced the outer steel; ten minutes of mental agony as they held their breath, with no way to be sure the silent alarms would not go off until the vault door was actually pulled open.

One of the two men spoke. Dressed in a black boiler suit and matching woolly hat, his few words were aimed at the man with the drill, and spoken in Russian.

'Ne zaderzhivaysya, khorosho?'

'It takes as long as it takes, Dimitri.'

Dimitri sucked in a nervous breath, turned away, and put a reassuring hand on the third man's shoulder. 'So far, so good, Sergei.'

Sergei nodded, walked a few steps to the fourth man, standing silently in the corner of the basement room, and spoke to him in English. 'Time for you and me to go back upstairs, Frank. You have done your job well, now we need to make it look like you haven't.'

The man turned and headed for the staircase. He wasn't dressed like the others, and he wasn't Russian either. Wearing the uniform of the night-security guard, he'd been employed by the bank for seven years; every one of those spent working a second job which no one knew about.

The foreigners he secretly worked for paid well, for a service that was rarely called-upon. But now, finally, it had been called. The payday bonus would be worth far more this time, for doing nothing other than turning the other cheek, and then allowing himself to be chloroformed into unconsciousness so his bosses and the police would never know he was an accomplice to the heist.

Money for nothing.

As Sergei and the security guard disappeared from his sight, Dimitri turned back to the vault door, and then glanced at his stopwatch. The drill-bit was halfway through the plating, right on the schedule they'd allowed for drilling. So far, things were going to plan.

He reached for the two black canvas bags, opened the zips. The bags were all but redundant for their true purpose of the heist, yet would play a major part in giving the robbery the appearance of any other bank job. He and his men were only there to steal one small item, but emptying a few other safety deposit boxes would make it look convincing... and be a nice bonus on the side.

He sucked in another nervous breath. There was nothing else to do until the drill had completed its work. Nothing to do but wait for the moment when all hell would break loose.

Two minutes later Sergei was back. 'It is done,' he said simply, pulling off his PVC gloves and discarding them in a corner. The man with the drill called out.

'Hey, Dimitri.'

It was time. The drill-bit parted from the door, and Sergei deftly inserted a steel rod into the hole, wrenching it firmly downwards. The three men heard a click, and Dimitri was on the move in less than a second, spinning the wheel of the opening mechanism so the other two could swing open the heavy old door.

There was no sound of alarms, but they all knew they were already going off at the Metropolitan Police HQ.

Within thirty seconds they were in the vault, the drill-man shoving a smaller bit into the drill and ripping out the safety deposit box locks, as the other two emptied the contents into the canvas bags. They already knew the number of the box they really wanted, but they drilled open a dozen others and took their contents too, just to make it look convincing.

Dimitri lifted the slim, oblong velvet box from the all-important tray, and smiled to himself as he opened the lid to make sure what they'd come for was inside. Then he threw it into one of the bags, and waved to the others. Their self-imposed two minute time limit was up.

The three men ran to the rope ladder dangling from the hole in the wall they'd made a half-hour earlier, climbed up to the empty M & S department store next door to the bank, hurried through the dark ground floor and slumped into the Audi waiting for them in the service road.

The driver sped away, but as the car turned into Pimlico High Street, he slowed to keep within the central London speed limit. As they drove slowly along the brightly-lit street, three police cars and their flashing blue lights screamed past them, heading the other way.

It wasn't difficult to work out where they were going.

Dimitri Novalenko smiled to himself as he glanced to the canvas bags on the seat beside him. The heist had been a great success, and a wrong had been righted.

Not everyone would see it that way, but he surely did.

It would be three days before he got the bad news. The heist might have been a success, but his sworn enemy Ilya Komanichov had outsmarted him. A week before, the man had ensured most of the world was aware he'd deposited the Crimson Heart in the vault... and now Dimitri knew exactly why he'd made it so public.

The massive and unique red diamond, flanked by silver angel wings, had been crafted into a pendant many years ago. It was beautiful, one of a very-expensive kind. But the one he'd just stolen was a fake. A very fine fake for sure, good enough to completely fool him. But it wasn't perfect enough to deceive his validation experts and their specialised equipment.

 He'd been well and truly, and deliberately, stung.

But the one thing Dimitri knew for sure was that the real Crimson Heart was somewhere in Ilya Komanichov's possession. And once he found out where he was hiding it, nothing and nobody would stand in the way of him getting it back.

———

Chapter 1

'Is that me?'

'It was taken when you were sixteen, nine years ago. I had it framed after you were… gone.'

'I do remember it, kind of. Looking at it now, it feels like I was someone else, watching me being photographed.'

Daisy smiled, put a loving arm around Celia's shoulder. 'It will come back to you. Give it a little time, and then you'll know for sure you're you.'

Celia was sitting on the bed in the room Daisy had made for her, the small framed photo of the three of them in her hands, her slightly-misty eyes transfixed onto it. It had only been half an hour since they'd arrived back at the cottage, waved goodbye to Sarah and the taxi which was continuing on to take her home, and wandered wearily into the house.

Celia was still more asleep than the others, but within fifteen minutes of arriving at her new home she was asking where she would sleep. Daisy had taken her upstairs to the room they'd furnished for their daughter. They hadn't even known for sure she was still alive, or if she would ever use it… but it had been made anyway.

She reached out a hand and wrapped it around her mother's. 'I can't believe you moved here and made a room for me… just in case.'

'It's called faith, dear. Although I will admit there were times it was hard to keep it.'

'I'm sorry, mum.'

Daisy pulled her into a hug. 'No need for that. None of it was your fault.'

'I'm getting vague flashes of things though… like before I was taken… when was it?'

'Just over three years ago.'

'Before I was taken, I feel misty memories that weren't so nice. But I can't actually see them, like they're in a thick fog.'

Daisy kissed her on her head. 'Now isn't the time to dwell on what happened back then. In a day or so, when you get used to your new surroundings, and if you want to, we'll jog your memory together. Right now, I want to just enjoy having you home safe.'

'Me too. It's a nice house; cosy somehow. I just wish I didn't feel like I could sleep forever.'

'Would you like to sleep now?'

Celia nodded. Daisy walked to the wardrobe, pulled open one of the doors. 'You may not want to wear any of this stuff anymore, but we kept all of it. For when you came home. Right now it's the sum total of what you've got, but when you feel up to it we'll hit the shops in Kings Lynn.'

'Thanks, mum. This is all a bit... overwhelming.'

Daisy hugged her again. 'Take your time. There really is no rush. Snuggle up, and your father and me are only in the next room if you need anything.'

'Thank you. For everything. I'm still not sure what you did apart from kidnapping me back, but something tells me it'll be jaw-dropping news when it comes.'

Daisy headed downstairs, her heart singing, but acutely aware one string was slightly out of tune. Before she'd left Celia she'd noticed her body was starting to shake again, part of the withdrawal symptoms from whatever it was Emmanuel Oyite was pumping into her for three years to make sure she stayed a willing submissive.

The Kenyan medics had given them a supply of medication to help combat the effects, but that was way short of enough fire-power in the long term. Much bigger guns were needed to fight the battle, and they were needed quickly.

'She's happy for now, dear,' Daisy said as she flopped wearily onto her stool at the peninsular unit in the kitchen area. 'But we can't wage that particular war alone.'

He handed her a large brandy. 'No, I realise that. It's early evening now, but tomorrow we'll contact the doc, and find a good clinic to get her detoxed.'

Daisy lowered her head. 'We've only just got her back, and I'm going to have to wave goodbye again?'

'Only for a couple of weeks. We can't do this without an expert helping hand, Flower.'

She let out a faltering sigh. 'I know. I wish I'd accepted that fact before Celia was taken. Now there's an even longer road ahead of us to defeat this particular villain.'

He took her hand, tried to smile some encouragement. 'Yes, but look on the bright side... everything we took to Uganda might have ended up exploding into a billion fragments, but the most precious thing of all didn't, and came back with us in one piece.'

'Just about, Dip.'

'So now it's down to us to make sure those pieces stay together.'

'You always were too sensible, dear.'

'I've had to find enough for both of us. But now it's seven in the evening, and we've just flown back from Africa in a less-than-comfortable transport aircraft. That bed of ours is screaming at me to fall into it. You mind if I do?'

'I'm right behind you.'

Still trying to force herself awake, Daisy wandered into the kitchen to find Aidan making coffee. Just about to wish him good morning, the patter of tiny feet on the gravel outside the kitchen door stopped the words forming.

It wasn't hard to work out there were four tiny feet, accompanied by two slightly bigger patters. A key was slipped into the lock, and the door opened to reveal the vision in polyester that was Maisie, with Brutus on the leash by her side.

She looked a little surprised she wasn't alone, to say the least. *'Daisy? Aidan?'* she stuttered.

'Coffee, Maisie?' Aidan grinned.

'What are you doing here?'

'Well we do live here,' said Daisy.

'But you're not due back for another four days... I think...' The short, slightly-portly woman counted on her fingers. 'Yes, four days it is. I was coming to water the plants, like you asked.'

'Let's just say we got done what we had to a little sooner than we expected,' said Aidan as he handed her a mug.

'But you said it was a holiday.' She took the mug, thanked him. 'Brutus is thirsty, can he have a saucer of milk? Semi-skimmed, mind you.'

Aidan shook his head, put the saucer of milk on the floor as Maisie unclipped the lead. The hairy furball looked grateful, even though once again he was the cat that didn't get the cream.

Daisy tried to offer an explanation for why they were back early, but was reluctant to go into too much detail. It *was* Maisie after all, who tended to need a little more careful explanation than most. 'It was a holiday, but there was another reason we went to Uganda as well.'

'Really? I don't suppose you're going to tell me tho...' The words trailed away as the reason they went to Africa wandered in, rubbing her eyes.

'Morning guys... oh, hello, whoever you are.'

Daisy grinned, even though she wasn't looking forward to the somewhat complicated introductions. 'Celia, this is Maisie. She's a bit nuts, but a really good friend.'

'*I beg your pardon?*'

'Maisie, this is Celia, my daughter.'

'Huh?'

'My daughter, Maisie... you know, fruit of my loins and all that?'

'I know what a daughter is, Daisy. I just didn't know you had one. Where have you been hiding her all this time?'

'We keep her locked away in the cellar. Seems like she just escaped.'

'Mum...'

'Daisy, I might be a little dozy but I'm not stupid. I know you don't have a cellar.'

Daisy, unable to resist winding up Maisie, who in truth did most of the winding-up all by herself, said something she likely shouldn't. 'Ah... it's a secret cellar. No one knows it's there except us.'

'*Mum...*'

'Oh I say... but isn't it illegal to keep someone locked away like that?'

Aidan was still shaking his head. 'Maisie, Daisy is just winding you up... again. We didn't lock our daughter away, but we did go to Africa to bring her back.'

'Oh I say. That takes a bit of believing, Aidan.'

Daisy put a hand on Maisie's arm. 'Actually dear, the truth is Celia was kidnapped three years ago, then trafficked to a Ugandan general who drugged her to keep her a submissive, then we got a clue about where she was from a Nigerian criminal who subsequently died, so we went to Africa to rescue her and almost caused an international incident, but we escaped to a tiny island where we got shelled by Howitzers which destroyed the home of an American hillbilly, then we were rescued by the Kenyan air force and flown back home in a British military transport aircraft.'

Maisie narrowed her eyes, and then grinned and batted her hand in front of her face. 'Daisy dear, if you're going to pull my chain, at least come up with something vaguely believable!'

'But it's the truth...'

Maisie shook her head and turned away. 'Perhaps you'll tell me what really happened one day. But I still can't see where the secret cellar fits in...'

She grabbed Brutus, ready to take her leave. Celia's sleep-filled eyes saw the furball for the first time. 'Aw... you've got a cat... *on a lead?*'

'Oh yes, dear,' said Maisie as she clipped the lead back onto his collar. 'He loves it when we go for a walk around the village. He's so good on the leash, and it stops him chasing the dogs.'

Daisy grinned. 'One day I'll tell you just how important Brutus was to finding you, Celia.'

She glanced to her father. 'This village seems like a very *interesting* place to live, dad.'

Maisie, much more switched-on than it first appeared, picked that up straightaway. *'Dad?* Now I'm really confused. Aren't you two just good friends?'

Daisy groaned. 'Maybe we'll just say we're friends with benefits... like a daughter.'

'Oh I say!' Maisie trotted through the kitchen door, the obedient Brutus by her side. 'I have to go now, before I get even more befuddled.' She disappeared, shaking her head.

Her parting words could still be heard though, just before she went out of listening range.

'Daisy Morrow and Aidan Henderson... well I never...'

Celia narrowed her eyes at her mother. 'Morrow... isn't that your maiden name, mum?'

Daisy groaned silently again. 'Dear, it's a long story. Shall we have breakfast first?'

Aidan picked up a small stack of post from the entrance hall just inside the front door, as Daisy tried to explain to Celia the reasons why she'd reverted to her maiden name when they moved to the village.

He came back into the kitchen, sorting the six letters in his hands. One of them was an A4 envelope, and as he looked at it curiously, he let out a chuckle.

'Dear?' said Daisy.

He showed her the envelope. She read the words printed right across the front. *'Open this if ye dare?'*

Aidan decided he was brave enough, and slid out a rectangle of stiff card with three pieces of paper attached to it, printed to look like old parchment.

'We've been invited to an all-expenses-paid two-day cruise on a pirate ship, dear,' he said quietly.

Daisy read through one of the invites. 'It's from Ilya Komanichov. Wasn't he the Russian tycoon you fell out with... what, almost twenty years ago?'

Aidan nodded. 'Yes. Just before I retired from the accountancy firm sixteen years ago, I voiced my suspicions to them that he was expecting us to... shall we say, be too creative with our accounting. They subsequently expelled him as a client.'

'And now he's inviting you on some kind of jolly?'

'Perhaps he wants to show me there were no hard feelings. It didn't exactly affect him... he's an oil billionaire now.'

'I know. He bought the rights to explore an oil field off the Norfolk coast, which came good. Made him a fortune once they started pumping the black stuff out.'

Aidan was reading the smaller print on the invite. 'It says he's built a full-size, fully-functioning replica of Jack Sparrow's ship, the *Black Pearl*, from the Pirates of the Caribbean movies. It's got twenty guest cabins, and he plans to operate it as a cruising hotel, recapturing the spirit of the pirate life.'

'For a small fortune in pieces of eight, no doubt. A bit like the one at Disneyworld, but this version actually sails.'

Celia was reading through her invite. 'It says the inaugural cruise departs from Great Yarmouth, and ends at its permanent home in London Docklands. And everyone on board has to wear pirate dress.'

Aidan smiled. 'It's four weeks from now. Maybe we should go, see it as a bit of therapy for Celia? Well, for us all perhaps.'

Daisy narrowed her eyes. 'Must confess I quite fancy waving a cutlass around for a couple of days.'

'Oh dear, dear. I forgot about the cutlass part.'

'Tell him we'll be delighted. But I'm a little curious as to why we're invited, after all this time.'

'Shall we just try and have a fun adventure without mortal danger involved for once, dear?

Chapter 2

Daisy was just swinging open the white five-barred gate to the drive, when someone swooped in with the honk of a handlebar horn, clearly thinking it had been opened for her.

The vision in red, a scarf knotted under her chin, and her cheeks almost as crimson as her coat, dropped a booted foot to the ground and slipped off the dark green and rather ancient ladies' bicycle like she had been riding side-saddle on a horse.

Then she fumbled in the red bag, and handed Daisy a folded piece of paper. 'There you go, Daisy Morrow. That's for you to sort.'

'Matilda, please take those stupid goggles off. You look like you're about to go for a swim. And I can't see your piggy eyes.'

Matilda threw her a glare from behind the blue swimming goggles, not that Daisy could see it very clearly. 'No remorse then I see, Daisy Morrow?'

Daisy sighed impatiently. Matilda was the last person she wanted to come face to face with that morning. 'Just Daisy will do. I am aware of my full name.'

Aidan, standing next to the car with Celia, shook his head and dropped into the driver's seat, deciding it was a girl thing and he was best leaving them to it. Celia however, unable to resist meeting another *interesting* village resident, wandered over as her mother began to unfold the piece of paper.

'What is it?' Daisy asked.

'It's the bill for the repairs and cleaning of my coat after you skittled me on your roller skates.'

Celia's eyes open wide. *'Roller skates?'*

Daisy groaned again. 'Another long story, dear. I'll tell you when there's more time.'

Matilda was a little keener to tell it right then. 'Yes. This... moron here decided to take up roller skating after her mobility scooter exploded into a million pieces.'

The eyes didn't get any smaller. 'Mobility scooter? *Exploded?*'

Luckily Matilda saved Daisy from any more awkward explanations. She finally lifted the goggles to her forehead, making her look like some kind of strange alien from *Tales of the Unexpected*, and looked curiously at Celia. 'And who are you anyway?'

Daisy, a little grateful for the distraction, made the introduction. Kind of. 'This is Celia. We just cloned her from Sarah... you know, that police woman friend of ours?'

Matilda narrowed her round eyes and peered a little closer. 'Hmm... you do look very like her... oh come on, Daisy Morrow. Seriously?'

'Mum...'

'*Mum?* Well I do declare!'

Daisy shook her head in frustration. She really could do without any more complications that particular morning. But it seemed there was no choice. 'This is our daughter. She's been in Africa for three years. She's with the Red Cross black ops squad.'

'*Mum...*'

'Yes dear, I know it's supposed to be a secret.'

'Red Cross bla... now you are pushing my belief window to its limits, Daisy Morrow.'

'I said just Daisy will suffice.'

'Stop trying to change the subject.'

'Ok, ok. The black ops unit infiltrates high-level corruption in Africa. Celia has been secretly investigating a

34

military general, who finally admitted his crimes but then lost his life. You don't mess with the Red Cross black ops division, trust me.'

'Well, I never.'

'Oh, Celia, this is Matilda, the village busyb... um, warden. She makes sure we all do things the way she... the way we should.'

Celia held out a hand, which Matilda shook vigorously. 'Well, I do hope you're not as disruptive as your mother. Just try and keep her within acceptable boundaries, please? This is a respectable village.'

Daisy grabbed the opportunity. 'Actually Matilda, Celia has just accepted another mission. Only two weeks this time, but if you don't mind she has to get there now, or she'll be late. I wasn't really opening the gate just for you.'

Matilda thrust the goggles back over her eyes, in a slightly deflated way. 'Very well, Daisy Morrow. Please settle that bill in the next seven days, or you'll have me to deal with.'

She threw her goggle-eyes to the sky, and then turned and wobbled out of the drive. Daisy watched the ancient bike careering away, which still had the beige fabric splash-guard fixed across the top of the rear wheel, and the original wicker basket on the front.

She waved to her in a slightly sarcastic way, even though Matilda's goggle-tunnelled vision could never see it.

'Enjoy your steampunk convention, Matilda,' she called after her, just as sarcastically.

'How many more crazy characters are there in this village... apart from *you*, mum?'

'You know what they say... you become like your peers,' Daisy grinned.

'Really? From what I've seen so far, they're becoming as crazy as you, not the other way round.'

'I shall take that as a compliment.'

They strolled back to the car, reached the passenger door. Daisy pulled her daughter into a tight hug. 'Be strong, hey? I know you can. We'll get through this, but it's really down to you to totally want to.'

'You know I do, mum. I caused you and dad grief even before I was taken. Those foggy memories are not so foggy now.'

Daisy felt her eyes misting up. She was being forced to say goodbye to the daughter she'd only just been reunited with, but it wasn't the only reason for the tears. The memories of the time before Celia was taken were far from foggy for Daisy.

'Are you sure you don't want me to come? I know I said I'd prefer to wish you well here rather than the unfamiliar surroundings of a clinic car park, but I will go with you.'

Celia took both of Daisy's hands in hers. 'No, I don't want you to come. In truth I would rather have gone on the train, but dad insisted on driving me. It's about owning this next two weeks, mum. Being the one who walks through the gate on her own two feet, with no one giving her a shove. Can you understand that?'

'One hundred percent, Celia,' said Daisy softly, never understanding anything so much in her life. 'And anyway, you really are a bit too old now for your parents to be dropping you at school! Now go, before I burst into tears.'

Celia pulled them into a tight hug again. 'I'm not sure I can ever thank you enough for what you did. But one way to help say it is to get myself clean... once and for all. I am strong now, mum. You and dad have given me back that strength, in just a few days. Think what we can do in a few months, together. But it starts with the next two weeks...'

Daisy opened the passenger door, held onto Celia's hand until the last possible moment. Aidan nodded silently to her, and she watched, a little misty-eyed, as the car drove out of sight.

She walked slowly back to the kitchen door, wiping away the tears with her thumbs. The family doctor had found Celia a place in a detox clinic, but it was the last placement they had, and the three of them needed to make a quick decision before it was taken by someone else.

For Daisy, in an ideal world it had come too soon. Celia had only been home four days, and waving goodbye again so quickly was a painful wrench. But it had to be, and Celia had really taken the decision for them, genuinely desperate to rid herself of the demons of addiction at the earliest opportunity.

It didn't make the parting any easier though. It *was* the right thing to do, but she knew there would be two weeks of hell in store for the daughter who had just gone through over three years of a different kind of hell. Somehow Daisy had needed more days of quiet reflection and recollection with Celia, before she was whisked away into the care of total strangers.

More days weren't to be. But as Daisy poured herself a brandy and sank onto her stool in the kitchen, she found her mind drifting into a quiet recollection of its own.

It was a bitter-sweet recall. Right then Celia was determined to do all she could to get herself clean. But three years ago, just before she was taken, and assisted by the insidious help of Jason Briggs, she'd refused to even acknowledge there was a problem.

It was a joyful thing Celia had now accepted demons lived inside her. But Daisy couldn't help wishing that when those demons had first reared their ugly heads, she'd ignored her daughter's protestations and forced her to get the help she was now desperate to find.

On the forty-mile drive to Norwich, Aidan filled his daughter in on her mother's dalliance with mobility scooters and roller skates.

He did his best to explain why, but it still sounded like his wife had gone a little crazier than she already was.

Celia, still shaking her head, seemed to think so too. 'I guess mum was always a bit off the wall,' she grinned.

'I think that's being a tad polite,' he answered, grateful that at least regaling Celia with tales of her mother's exploits had taken her mind off their eventual destination.

The journey seemed way to short. As Aidan pulled into the car park, he glanced to Celia. 'I guess you don't want me to escort you to reception?'

'No way, thanks all the same, dad. I'm going to walk in there with my head held high, and then walk out in two weeks time with it held even higher.'

He gave her a hug. 'That's my girl. Your mother may be out of the box, but she gave you her fighting spirit.'

Celia nodded, a little sadly. 'I know. I just wish I'd been able to accept that before... before I was taken.'

He took her hand. 'Hey, the past is dead and gone. What matters now is the future. And your mother and I can give you all the love and support possible, but ultimately it's up to you. And we both know you can do it, and that you'll walk out of there a couple of inches taller than when you went in.'

'You always manage to say the right thing, dad.'

'I can't help having a brain the size of a small galaxy.'

She laughed. 'I guess that's a mum-ism?'

'What do you think?'

She kissed him on the cheek. 'Just keep doing it.' She reached to the rear seat for her case, and then walked the thirty yards to the entrance door, turned and waved, and was gone.

Aidan sat unmoving for a few minutes, the same conflicting emotions running through his mind as had drifted across Daisy's a short while before.

For sure in one way it had come too soon. But in another, it couldn't have come soon enough.

Chapter 3

'Not another wig?'

Daisy spun round on the dressing table stool, and flicked her flowing red locks like she was really proud of them. 'Don't you think it suits me, dear?'

He grinned. 'I prefer you with silver hair. But I guess it goes with the character.'

'Anne Bonny was flame-haired, by all accounts.'

'You do know she was having intimate relations with Mary Read... by all accounts?'

Daisy reached out, took Aidan's hand. 'Yes, but the love of her life was Calico Jack... which is why I suggested you go as the flamboyant pirate, dear.'

He glanced down at the baggy pink pantaloons. 'Not at all sure about the colour, though.'

'Dip, Calico Jack got his name because of his outrageously colourful outfits... and anyway, pink quite suits you.'

'Is that a compliment or an insult?'

She kissed his hand with a slightly wicked smile. 'You decide.'

Daisy turned back to the mirror, tied the red bandana-style scarf around her head, and stood up to give Aidan a twirl. He let out an impressed whistle, acknowledging the fact she actually did look rather awesome in the dark-green pantaloons tucked inside long brown boots, the wide matching belt around her waist, a man's white shirt tied at the neck with black strings, and the long red velvet coat with its bold brass buttons.

'All I need now is a scabbard with a very sharp sword in it,' she grinned.

'Let's just leave the *very sharp* bit out of that, ok?'

Daisy looked Calico Jack up and down. His baggy pantaloons were tucked inside red boots, and pulled in at the waist by a swath of red fabric, patterned with gold fleur de leys. His shirt was deep ochre, and covered with a long, flowing waistcoat-type jacket. On his head he sported the thin, brown tri-corn hat favoured by pirate captains of the time.

'You should dye your hairy facial bits honey-blonde, dear,' she grinned. 'By all accounts Calico was golden-haired.'

They were trying on their costumes for the cruise. Still almost three weeks to departure, Daisy needed a distraction from Celia's absence, and the day after she'd left, got onto procuring the best costumes she could. There had to be plenty going on to take her mind off the somewhat harsh reality of the no-nonsense treatment their daughter was enduring.

Hers and Aidan's costumes had just arrived. Celia's was going to take a while longer. Daisy had contacted the seamstress who made her wedding dress thirty-five years ago. A young woman back then just starting her business, Daisy had clicked right away with her approach to life, and commissioned her to make the outfit for her big day.

Not into frills and fancies, the long, sheer cream wedding dress was relatively plain and simple, but totally beautiful and a perfect fit. They'd stayed in touch over the years, and as Audrey was still doing her thing now, she made the obvious choice to help with the forthcoming event.

It wasn't initially about their two costumes; it was to do with Celia's. Daisy wanted something really special, a thank

41

you gift for what Celia was willingly putting herself through; something to make her feel like a million dollars after she came out the other side. When she'd said she wanted to go on the cruise as Elizabeth Swann, there was only one dress she could wear.

The dress.

When Daisy had spoken to Audrey about it, and sent her a picture of the dress, she'd agreed to make it, but warned her it wouldn't be cheap. Aidan has raised his eyebrows when Daisy showed him the quote, but after she'd frowned her annoyance and asked him if their daughter was worth it, he'd said the only truth he could.

'Of course she is, dear. Every penny.'

Daisy had told Audrey to go ahead and make the iconic gold dress, and she'd offered to create their costumes too, for a discounted all-in price. Needless to say, Daisy agreed.

Eight days after she said goodbye again to Celia, hers and Aidan's costumes arrived. The dress itself would be another week, delivered just after Celia got home from the clinic.

They both wanted it to be a very special welcome-home surprise.

'Ok dear, we both look awe-inspiring. Time to take it all off now, and save it for the big day. And procure ourselves a couple of swords as well, of course.'

'*Imitation* swords, Flower.'

'Of course, dear.'

Aidan followed Daisy downstairs to the bar stools, made them both a strong coffee. He knew all too well why Daisy was filling her time with preparations for the pirate cruise, even though there was more time than she really needed to have everything sorted.

She'd spent some of those days poring over the fine detail of Celia's dress with Audrey... more than she'd spent poring over her own wedding dress, if the truth were told. It had taken away some of the endless hours she would otherwise have spent fretting.

The poring had helped, but not entirely. Daisy's sleep patterns were erratic and disturbed, and a big part of that was because she blamed herself for their daughter getting taken in the first place. Aidan knew it wasn't her fault, but he also knew the fraught emotions of the night she was abducted hadn't helped.

Neither of them were there when Celia was taken. And given the volatile situation on that awful night, Aidan was perhaps just as much to blame, if there was ever blame to attach at all.

Trying to be there for two out-of-control family members had proved to be impossible.

They'd been allowed a short visit to the clinic the previous day. That too had helped, but not totally. Their daughter looked drawn, and was clearly going through her own personal hell. But she also looked bright-eyed, and was positive about how she was being treated.

Just before they left she told them it was the best thing she'd ever done, and how much she wished she'd been able to accept an intervention before.

Daisy hugged her and smiled, knowing just how true those words were, for them both. On the way out they'd sat down with the chief consultant, who told them Celia was doing extremely well, and he and his staff believed the original two-week stay would not have to be extended.

Then his face grew a little more sombre, and he warned them that people who had been reliant on substances for

43

an extended time had a habit of appearing like they'd been cured, but that fifty-percent of them ended up succumbing to their demons once again.

It was a bitter-sweet trip for them both. Joyful to see Celia so positive, but then reminded that a two-week stay in a detox clinic was just the start of the journey, not the final destination.

Daisy sipped her coffee, deep in thought. But this time it wasn't about Celia. 'Shall we get the flowers on the way in the morning, dear?' she asked quietly.

'I think that's best. I'm about to down a midday brandy now, so better not use the car again today.'

'Yes, dear. You struggle to keep a straight line at the best of times.'

'I shall definitely take *that* as an insult.'

They'd decided to make another trip the next day. Once again it was something they wished they didn't have to do, but something they needed to do regardless.

There had not really been time before then. A short trip to Belgium and a longer one to Africa had meant there was no chance of doing one of the things they really wanted to do.

Something else that was likely to spark yet more emotions, none of them good.

Chapter 4

When they reached the cemetery in Kings Lynn, someone else was already at the graveside.

'Sarah?'

The young police woman scrambled to her feet, looked slightly embarrassed. 'Guys... I wasn't expecting to see you here.'

Daisy glanced at the posy of flowers sat in a small glass vase on the grave. 'We've come to do what I guess you've just done, Sarah.'

She lowered her head. 'I... I know it's not the done thing, police officers putting flowers on a victim's grave, but...'

Daisy pulled her into a hug. 'Maybe so, but it's a lovely thing to do, nevertheless.'

Sarah wiped away a tear. 'I just felt so bad. He was a totally innocent victim, and apart from anything else, if it hadn't been him, it would have been...' The words faded into a quiet sob.

Aidan put a consoling hand on her shoulder. 'Tragically, we're all too aware that but for the grace of whoever is up there, it would have been Daisy.'

Daisy lifted her eyes to the sky, blinked away her own tears. 'There's something else we have to be eternally grateful to Bob for.'

'What's that?'

'Because he lost his life instead of me, investigating who had actually got it in for me and killed him instead, led directly to us finding Celia. This is an awful thing to have to admit, but if Bob hadn't died we likely would never have found our daughter. We owe him more than just the obvious.'

Sarah turned away, nodded her head. 'I have to go now. I just called in on my way to the station. I'm so glad you two are here... to say hi to Bob, and thank him for what he never knew he did.'

'Count on it, Sarah. It's just about the first chance we've had, what with getting Celia sorted and all.'

'How is she doing?'

Aidan found a smile. 'Good. We were allowed a short visit the day before yesterday. She looked drained but positive and determined. They're putting her through the mill, but she's set on seeing it through.'

'I'm so happy for her. And you two... you kind of went through hell to bring her back.'

Daisy gave her a final hug. 'And so did you, my girl. I hate to think what would have happened if you hadn't been there to sort out my crazy, impetuous antics.'

'It *was* your daughter, Daisy.'

'Tell that to Aidan. He still thinks I went even more insane that usual.'

Sarah grinned. 'He's not wrong there. But now and again there are exceptional circumstances.'

'You listening, dear?'

'Of course, Flower.'

Sarah giggled at her friend's banter. 'I wish I was coming with you on the Black Pearl. It sounds so exciting!'

'Let's hope not too exciting. I'm sure Aidan could swing you an invite if you like?'

'Oh... no, I'm on duty that weekend, and I've just had two weeks leave. Don't think Burrows would be too impressed. But I'm going to get you to send me blow-by-blow photos... every two hours, mind!'

'Consider it done, Sarah dear.'

She waved a hand as she headed back to the car park. Daisy knelt down, placed the elegant bone-china vase she was holding onto the flat granite of the grave, and Aidan dropped beside her and arranged the flowers into it. She slipped her hand into his as she spoke softly to the man she hoped could somehow hear the words.

'Bob, these flowers are the first of many, because as long as Aidan and me walk this Earth, we'll make sure there are fresh ones here for you every month. You never knew what you did for us, at huge cost to yourself and your family, but I hope somehow you can hear my voice, because I'm telling you now your sacrifice hurts us all like hell, but then in a different way you could never have imagined, brought us joy.

'In my life I have seen death more times than I care to recall, but here today I can honestly say no one person's has ever meant so much. Through a quirk of fate you lie there now instead of me, and I can't tell you how dreadful that makes me feel...'

The words faded into tears. Aidan curled an arm around her shoulders, and finished what he knew she wanted to say. 'But tragic as it was, your loss became our gain, and we both know if you can hear these heartfelt words, it will bring a smile to your face because it did. Thank you Bob, in so many ways.'

Five days later Daisy and Aidan sat in the BMW together, waiting impatiently for Celia to walk through the door from the clinic, a couple of inches taller than when she went in.

This time Daisy couldn't help but keep Aidan company, and as their daughter appeared, she also couldn't help sprinting across the gravel and almost knocking her over as she pulled them close.

47

'*Mum...*'

'Sorry. No one's watching though. Not even a teacher.'

'I forgive you.'

Daisy finally stepped back a little. 'Look at you, all glowing and gorgeous.'

'Hardly... I feel a wreck, and I still want to sleep for England.' An uncertain frown creased her mother's forehead, made her laugh. 'Don't worry, I'm fine. Just take me home please, so I can be where I belong, with people I love.'

Daisy took her hand, and together they sank into the rear seat. 'Drive us home please, Henderson. And don't hang about!'

'Yes, ma'ams,' he grinned, and threw the car into reverse. Daisy looked at Celia. 'So how was it... honestly?'

She nodded and shook her head all at the same time. 'Honestly, it was hell. But the kind of hell that's somehow got heaven in sight at the end of it. I did learn one huge lesson though.'

'What's that?'

'I don't ever want to go there again!'

Chapter 5

Two days after Celia got home, a parcel arrived for her. She was still asleep when the delivery driver dropped it off, and Aidan had to stop an excited Daisy from waking her right there and then.

Luckily a smaller parcel arrived too, which gave Daisy something to open for Christmas.

She pulled the two scabbards from the box, and carefully made sure she gave Aidan the one that was his. He slid the imitation sword from its sheath, swished it around in the air, and then felt the blade.

'Cool cutlass, dear... nicely balanced, but it's as blunt as hell. Is yours the same?'

She slid it part way out of its holder, but didn't let it see the light of day any further. 'Of course, Calico. Just the kind of thing a female pirate would possess. Now can I go wake Celia?'

Aidan was about to ask if he could see the sword anyway, but then Celia interrupted his train of thought, padding into the living room and spotting the box on the peninsular unit.

'Oh, wow. *Is that my dress?*' she shrieked.

'Can't imagine it's anything else, addressed to you,' said Daisy slightly nervously, and in a somewhat relieved way as she put both the swords back into the box.

Celia ran a kitchen knife through the tape holding the dress box together, and folded back the flaps. Then she parted the thin foam wrapping, and gasped. '*Mum... dad...* you told me you'd arranged a dress for me, but *this*...'

49

She lifted the iconic gold dress from the box, in an awestruck kind of way. 'This is unbelievably cool... and it must have cost a lot of... pieces of eight.'

'Worth every piece, dear,' Daisy breathed, just as awestruck by her daughter's reaction.

Celia unfolded the dress, and let it drop to its full golden splendour as she held it up. 'Mum... it's beautiful. And lighter than I imagined.'

Daisy smiled. 'It's made predominately from silk taffeta, just like it would have been back then. Otherwise all those folds and acres of fabric would have felt like wearing a suit of armour.'

Celia was still shaking her head. 'Just look at the... middle bit...'

'Stomacher.'

'It's all jewelled... so intricate. And you've even sorted the shoes too, with the silk flowers.'

'Well, you could hardly go in a pair of Sketchers. We studied all the photographs. Ok, we pored over them for hours if the truth is told. We all thought if you're going to wear such an iconic dress it had to be spot on.'

'And you do look a bit like Keira Knightly,' said Aidan.

'Can I go try it on?'

'I was just about to drag you upstairs,' Daisy grinned.

Celia was already heading into the hallway as she called back, 'No need... give me five.'

Daisy took the opportunity to stash the box containing the swords in the office, and then took up her customary position back on the bar stool. They heard the footsteps on the stairs, and Daisy drew a deep breath.

And then, in all her glory, Elizabeth Swann was there.

'*Oh my...*' Daisy exhaled the breath she hadn't been able to release for at least a minute. Aidan ran a silent hand across his mouth, unable to utter anything at all.

Their daughter looked incredible.

She smiled a beautiful smile. 'Apart from the fact I feel like I'm just about to go to my first prom... will I do?'

Daisy almost staggered over, wrapped her arms around her. '*Do..?* You look... magnificent... Elizabeth.'

'I still can't believe you did all this for me.'

'Seeing you looking like that, after everything you've been through...' Daisy turned away, covered her face with her hands.

'Mum... you'll get me going if you're not careful.'

Aidan kissed Celia gently on the cheek. 'Suddenly I'm envious of Will Turner. Beautiful.'

Celia wiped away the mistiness. 'I told you you'd get me going. But I want you guys to know something. Mum, look at me please?'

Daisy turned to her daughter, half-laughed, half-sobbed. 'I'm looking, dear.'

'This dress, stunning though it is, is really just a few yards of taffeta and sequins. But what it *means* is the most important thing to me. We've all been through different kinds of hell in the last three or four years, but I know why you guys have gone to all this trouble. This dress marks the closure of a time we all want to forget, but it also marks the beginning of a new era... for you and for me.'

'So you're going to Swann off, marry a blacksmith's son, and sail the seven seas as a pirate queen?' Daisy sniffed.

Celia giggled. 'Well, I don't know about that. But as soon as I put it on I felt a rush of gratitude and joy... not just for the dress, but for having you two as the solid foundation of a family that didn't take no for an answer. Wearing this is

51

like saying the biggest thank you in the universe, and something that spurs me on to never let this incredible family down again.'

Daisy buried her face in Celia's shoulder. 'Then it's achieved everything we hoped it would.'

Aidan pulled them into a group hug. 'I suppose Ilya's pirate cruise invitation could not have come at a more opportune moment.'

Celia laughed, kissed him on the forehead. 'Dad, your galactic-sized brain doesn't need me to confirm that.'

'Now I'm starting to wish I was going as Elizabeth's father in the movie.'

Daisy narrowed her eyes at him. 'Over my dead body. In that stupid curly wig?'

Chapter 6

'I thought the Great Yarmouth Maritime Festival was last month?'

'So you think having the Black Pearl sitting in the harbour isn't just as much of an attraction?'

'Judging by the massing throngs, it's even more of a crowd-puller.'

They had plenty of time to see, and a perfect view of the scene. Crawling across the Haven Bridge at virtually zero miles an hour in a hardly-moving queue of traffic, the incredible sight just over to their right was unlike anything Great Yarmouth had seen before.

The Black Pearl was moored against the harbour wall, a hundred yards before the bridge. Her black sails were furled, the tall masts sitting higher than the bridge itself. The wide quay, and the harbour road just beyond it, was a pulsing mass of humanity. Hundreds of people had turned out to see the iconic ship begin its journey to London.

As they crawled over the bridge, they could make out that even some of the onlookers were in costume. Ilya Komanichov, whether deliberately or not, had done a very good job of making sure everyone knew about his latest venture.

Aidan dropped the driver's window, and suddenly they could hear the cinematic music from the movie franchise booming out from big speakers positioned on the dockside, adding a perfect soundtrack to the scene.

Someone however, didn't seem so happy. They heard a small voice from the rear seat. 'There's too many people. I'm not used to lots of people...'

Daisy reached back and slipped her hand in Celia's. 'Hey, it'll be ok. Once we get through the throng there won't be so many people on board. Be strong.'

'It's the throng that worries me. Especially in this dress.'

Aidan turned and smiled. 'Don't worry... we'll use our swords if we have to stop anyone getting too close.'

'Thank you, dad.'

'Actually, I wasn't being...'

Daisy put a hand on his arm. 'Dear, remember who you are.'

'You mean Celia's father, or Calico Jack?'

'Both.'

They finally made it to the narrow street on the other side of the town hall, which ran parallel to the harbour road just the other side of the buildings. Their host had booked an entire small car park a little way along, for the exclusive use of his guests.

As Aidan turned into the entrance they were met by a bearded pirate, who asked to see their invites, and then suggested they park up and use the tiny connecting road to get to the harbour, as it would be a little less crowded.

Celia looked grateful for his words, but as they made the harbour, a little less crowded seemed like wishful thinking. Two runs of temporary metal barriers did their best to form a pathway for the guests through the massing throngs, but the barriers were struggling to keep the marauders at bay.

Daisy and Aidan flanked their daughter as she began to look overwhelmed by all the attention, not exactly helped by the amazing dress. It seemed like a million cameras were firing off, and at least three TV cameras followed their path as they made their way towards the towering black ship.

'Give us a kiss, Elizabeth...' someone shouted.

Celia kept her head down, as Daisy brandished her sword at the guy, making the crowd laugh. Then finally they were through the gauntlet, and the Oscar catwalk opened out to a bigger, less crowded space right in front of the ship, guarded by ten rather large security bouncers.

A small crowd of costumed guests were gathered close to the gangplank. Daisy shook her head. 'Look at them, dears. Almost every man looks like a navy commander, and every woman looks like a high society floosie.'

Aidan grinned. 'I guess Ilya's rich pals weren't going to go as common pirates... and the women are supposed to be eighteenth-century *ladies*, dear.'

'Hmm... so why don't any of them look as good as our daughter then?'

'Can we just get aboard?' asked Celia, looking like she'd already had enough.

They headed for the gangplank, but just before they made it, someone turned and spotted them. Their host smiled broadly through the whiskers and the beard as he walked up to them.

'My dears... you made it. Please accept my apologies for the huge crowds. I did not expect...'

Aidan looked the man over. He was every bit who he was purporting to be. 'Ilya... I suppose I should have anticipated you would be Barbossa.'

The Russian laughed. 'Who else, my friend?' He raised his eyebrows to Celia. 'You have indeed grown into a vision of beautiful splendour, Celia. My ship is truly dedicated to you, and you alone.'

She lifted her eyes, forced a smile. 'Thank you, Captain Barbossa. And you indeed are the perfect replica of a true pirate captain.'

Then Jack Sparrow was there, complete with blackened eyes and beaded beard. 'If I may intercede a moment, I should make a small point of some relevance...'

'What do you want, Jack Sparrow?' barked Barbossa impatiently.

'*Captain* Jack Sparrow, if you please. And my small but relevant point is that by the rules of international maritime law, the captain of said ship must be... um... alive.'

'Are you suggesting my *undead* status is relevant here, Jack?'

Jack grinned. 'Just making a small but relevant point, Barbossa.'

He wandered off to play his role to another group of guests. Daisy shook her head. 'He even sounds like Jack Sparrow, Ilya. Well done there.'

'Yes... I spend a not inconsiderable amount of time choosing the right actor. He will be the centre of attention this weekend, after all. Sadly, Johnny Depp was not interested.'

'I guess he wouldn't be, even though he owns a house in Norfolk. I don't think the franchise really wants him anymore.'

He laughed. 'Indeed.' He looked Daisy up and down. 'And you, dear lady, are the infamous Anne Bonny, I assume?'

'One and the same. This is my lover... Calico Jack Rackham.'

'A fitting choice. Did you know they have just written a new script for the Pirates of the Caribbean series, this time with two women in the lead roles... one of them with flame hair?'

'I did know, yes.'

'Let us hope it will be made. However, now it is time to board. We depart in half an hour. Come...'

He led the way to the gangplank, which was made to look like ancient wood but had a double safety rail to make sure his rich guests didn't fall off, and then beckoned to the other guests to follow. Daisy glanced to Celia and Aidan as she put a foot on the boarding ladder.

'Let's hope we're not walking the plank already, hey guys?'

Chapter 7

The Black Pearl felt every bit like the iconic pirate ship she was pretending to be. Daisy glanced around as they reached the deck, trying to find something that didn't belong in the eighteenth century.

She could see nothing out of place. Everything from the rigging to the capstans seemed real.

'Your friend has done a good job, dear,' she whispered to Aidan. 'Do you think we'll be sleeping in hammocks?'

'I hope not. My back wouldn't like that very much.'

'Don't be such a wuss. If we do, it'll be part of the experience.'

They weren't to find out for a short while. As the other guests made their way aboard, one of the crew who looked a bit like Mr. Gibbs asked them to remain on deck until the ship had departed, so those on the quayside who were photographing and filming got the money shots as the ship sailed away. Captain Barbossa was about to say a few words as well, to fill his guests in on what to expect over the next two days.

Then the music booming out through the speakers fell silent, and a brass band dressed in the red and white soldiers uniforms of the period began to assemble on the quayside as the gangplank was withdrawn. Captain Barbossa, with Jack Sparrow by his side, stepped up to the raised roof of the quarterdeck, and addressed his guests.

'Ladies and gentlemen, welcome to the maiden voyage of the Black Pearl. As you can see, she is a magnificent replica of the famous ship, accurate in every detail, and built at vast expense. It has to be said, it would have been cheaper to build a considerably larger modern vessel than the one hundred and sixty-five feet of painstakingly-crafted wooden delight you see here. However, that was not the objective. I have been fascinated by pirates from a very young age...'

'*I bet you have...*' said Daisy under her breath.

'...and now I have business interests in this part of the world, it is only fitting that the inaugural cruise of my pride and joy begins in Great Yarmouth. In two weeks time she will begin taking a small number of guests on two-day cruises...'

'At great expense,' butted in Jack, waggling a finger, to a murmur of laughter from the guests.

'At a *bargain price* for the experience, from her permanent home in the docklands of London,' Ilya continued, with a sideways glance to Jack. 'As you can see we have cut no corners above decks to ensure an accurate eighteenth-century experience for you all. However, below decks we have taken a few liberties to make life more comfortable. I assure you that you will not be sleeping in hammocks.'

The guests laughed again, in a relieved kind of way. Aidan grinned to Daisy. 'That's my back sorted then.'

'The gun deck, immediately below you, has been converted to eighteen double cabins, nine on each side. Two further, and more luxurious cabins have been built in the forecastle towards the bows, and for this voyage only, will be occupied by myself and Jack.

'Although you will find your accommodation very comfortable, it has still been designed in the style of the period. For instance, all lighting is by oil lamps and candles...not real ones of course, modern regulations would not allow it, especially with all this wood around. But you will be hard-pressed to know they are imitation.'

He indicated the quarterdeck at his feet. 'Below me, what would have been the captain's suite and reception rooms have been converted to your dining and recreation area, and styled in the manner of the Tortuga bar. There are tables where you will take your meals... knives and forks supplied if required... and a small bar for alcoholic drinks.'

'Rum, rum, and... oh, more rum,' said Jack with a Sparrow-type swagger. The guests cheered.

Barbossa shook his head. 'Below the gun deck, and off limits for guests, the guts of the ship are however extremely modern. Whilst we will sail in the traditional manner where possible, out of sight there are two caterpillar diesels for additional propulsion, and generators for electrical power.

'Also located there is the computer that controls all systems, and various other things we have to carry to stay within regulations. This cannot be avoided, but none of it will be visible to spoil your experience. There are fourteen crew members aboard, eight to sail the ship, six to look after your every need. We wish all of you will embrace the experience, and hope you enjoy the next two days in their true spirit, as the guests of a pirate crew.'

A cheer went up from the small crowd, and it seemed they all agreed embracing the experience as instructed was a good idea. Their captain waved an arm in the air. 'Mr. Gibbs, it is time to unfurl the sails, so that we may be on our way. Let the journey commence!'

The rush of anticipation could almost be heard from the guests, but Barbossa hadn't quite finished. 'Oh, and as soon as we leave harbour, we have a little brief entertainment for you. Once you have settled into your cabins and before lunch is served, Jack Sparrow and Will Turner will re-enact their first swordfight for your pleasure. Enjoy!'

Three crew members began to scale the rigging to unfurl the sails, and the band on the quayside struck up, a rendition of 'We are Sailing'... of course. The Lord Mayor of Yarmouth appeared from nowhere, and the massed crowd began to cheer as two other pirates slipped the mooring lines from the iron bollards.

Several hundred Union Jack flags started waving, and as the ship moved sideways away from the quay, assisted by very modern side-thrusters, the guests piled to the starboard side of the ship to wave to the masses.

The black ship turned slowly in a half-circle, pointing towards the open sea. A gentle wind filled the sails, and she began to move forward.

Daisy looked at Aidan and Celia, as the sound of the wind in the sails and the creaking of the rigging immediately took them back a couple of centuries. 'We're off, me hearties,' she whispered. 'For better or for worse.'

'Maybe we'll leave the worse bit out of that sentence for once, hey dear?' said Aidan.

'I just want to enjoy being Elizabeth Swann,' said Celia, a smile back on her face now the massing crowds were behind them.

'Absolutely. Now you're on the Black Pearl, you really are her. Let's go find our cabins, shall we?' said Daisy, trying to shake off the slightly negative vibes that just didn't seem to want to be shaken off.

They headed for the opening to the hold, which wasn't a hold anymore, and now had a proper wooden staircase instead of a rope ladder. Then Captain Barbossa appeared, and caught Aidan's arm.

'A little later, come and see me in my quarters please, my friend? We have a lot of catching up to do.'

Aidan nodded, wondering what *catching up* meant. 'After the entertainment, Ilya, ok?'

'Of course. Settle yourself in, and then we will talk.'

Daisy shook her head as they headed down the steps to a long, oak-lined corridor with the doors to the guest cabins branching off each side. Aidan and Celia were determined to enjoy the better, but she couldn't help feeling the worse wasn't that far away.

Chapter 8

Each of the guest cabins had a tiny gold plaque on the door, with their names etched into it in black letters.

Aidan turned the matching gold knob, and as he swung the door ajar his eyes opened wide.

'We've got a cannon, dear!' he exclaimed.

They had got a cannon. A real, full-size iron and wooden cannon sat proudly in the room, its barrel pointing through the gun port to the outside world.

'Well, I suppose it is the gun deck, dear,' said Daisy.

'Won't it be a bit draughty out at sea?' Aidan walked over, ran his hand along the barrel. 'Oh, I see.'

'You see?'

'The gun port is a glass window, with a hole in it for the barrel to poke through.'

'Nice touch.' Daisy pointed to a low four-sided open box next to the cannon. 'There are cannonballs too!'

'Now dear, don't go getting any ideas.'

'Funny guy.'

Daisy's eyes flicked around the room, drinking in the ambience. Their decent-sized quarters were capped by a low, beamed ceiling, which looked like it really had been made from three-hundred year old timbers. On one wall, a chunky four-poster bed was draped with red and green fabric, and two low bedside tables supported pseudo oil lamps, flickering away just like oil lamps should.

The walls were wood-panelled too, with gold-leaf picture frames surrounding portraits of famous pirates. A red carpet covered the floor, and on the rear wall a dressing table with an ornate mirror sat between two elaborately-sculpted wardrobes, their doors adorned with gold detailing.

A door led to a small en suite, which wasn't exactly eighteenth century, but did its best to disguise the modern power-shower unit and flush toilet.

"Well dear, at least we won't have to go in a bucket and throw it over the side,' Daisy grinned.

'According to you that would have been all part of the experience,' said Aidan.

'That's one version of *experience* I could do without,' she growled.

A small chaise-longue completed the opulent look, with a low weathered-oak table in front of it. Aidan picked up the triple candle-holder sitting on it, the three candles burning away.

'Don't burn your fingers,' Daisy quipped.

Aidan studied the fake flames. 'It's amazing. They look just like real flame.'

'As I said, don't burn your fingers,' Daisy repeated.

'Why do I get the feeling you're not actually referring to fingers?'

Daisy pulled him into a hug, didn't answer the question directly. 'I wonder what Ilya wants to talk to you about?'

'No idea. But I'm curious to find out.'

Daisy was about to say something, but the door opened and an excited Celia almost ran in. 'Oh... you've got a cannon too! How amazing is this?'

'It's pretty special. I feel like a very privileged pirate.'

'You are. And I feel like a real-life Elizabeth Swann. Thank you so much, guys.'

Aidan smiled. 'Perhaps you should thank Ilya. This whole weekend is a freebie after all.'

'I will when I see him. And in a minute I get to see Will and Jack fencing it out too.'

'Look at you, all flushed and excited,' Daisy grinned.

'Mum, I meant... well, you know what I mean.'

'So why do I get a feeling of movie déjà vu?'

'Mum...'

'From what I've seen already, Ilya will have chosen someone to play Will who is young, handsome and dashing.'

'*Mum...*'

Aidan shook his head as he grinned wickedly. 'We *are* all supposed to get in the spirit of the moment, Celia.'

'Dad, are you winding me up again?'

'Looking like that, I'm not so sure I am.'

Daisy slipped an arm into his. 'Dear, leave the matchmaking to the girls. But I will admit, from what I've seen of our guests, all the other women look like saggy dowagers.'

'Mum!'

'Just saying it like it is, dear.'

Celia was about to utter a barrage of false protests, but a tuneful ping coming from hidden speakers stopped the words in their tracks. Captain Barbossa's voice filled the room.

'Arr me hearties, methinks there might be a duel to the death about to happen on deck. If ye wish to witness the fight of the century, I suggest ye come topsides, at the double!'

Daisy grinned. 'Well dears, it's time to find out just how handsome and dashing Will Turner really is.'

'Mum...'

65

Chapter 9

Will Turner did possess a fairly close resemblance to Orlando Bloom. Once again Ilya had chosen carefully, and Daisy's feeling of movie déjà vu wasn't going away.

'He is quite dashing and handsome,' Daisy whispered.

'Mum... stop it.'

The guests had been directed to the forward part of the main deck, where temporary ropes prevented them from going any further towards the rear quarterdeck. Gathered around the three lifeboats covered by ancient-looking but very new tarpaulins, which concealed the fact regulations had demanded the lifeboats were somewhat newer than eighteenth-century, they watched as Jack hid himself behind the main mast, and Will appeared above them on the quarterdeck.

He took off his long coat as he walked down the steps to the main deck, revealing the brown waistcoat and white shirt they all knew so well. A sword lay on one of the spokes of the capstan wrapping around the foot of the mast, and as Will headed over to it, he frowned.

'*Not where I left you,*' he said as he reached out for it, the exact words his counterpart used in the movie.

Just before his hand closed around the hilt, Jack revealed himself, slapping the flat side of his sword onto Will's wrist. He drew his hand away, looked up with wide eyes.

'*You're the one they're hunting. The pirate.*'

Jack peered at him, looked a little curious. '*You seem somewhat familiar. Have I threatened you before?*'

'*I make it a point to avoid familiarity with pirates.*'

'*Ah. Then it would be a shame to put a black mark on your record. If you'll excuse me...*'

Jack started to walk away, make his escape. But Will had other ideas, grabbed the sword and pointed it at Jack, who didn't exactly look impressed.

'Do you think this is wise, boy? Crossing blades with a pirate?'

'You threatened Miss Swann.'

'Only a little.'

'They're talking about me,' said Celia quietly, only a tiny bit flushed around the cheeks.

It was pretty clear to Jack that Will wasn't going to let him escape without a fight. He lunged, but was parried. The two swords clashed, glinting in the light of the midday sun, as both of them tried to outdo the other, moving around the deck in a circle as they fought desperately for their lives.

Then Jack pulled back a little, smiled to Will. *'You know what you're doing, I'll give you that. But how's your footwork?'*

Will did a silly dance, and a very athletic twirl, to show his opponent just how good his footwork was. The guests laughed, but Will still had a determined look on his face.

'I practice three hours a day.'

'You need to find yourself a girl, mate. Or, perhaps the reason you practice three hours a day is that you've already found one, and you're otherwise incapable of wooing said strumpet. You're not a eunuch are you?'

That didn't seem to sit too easily with Will. He slashed at Jack, who parried him again. Then, swords crossed and temporarily motionless, their faces were just two feet apart.

'I practice three hours a day so that when I meet a pirate, I can kill him.'

Jack thrust him away, lashed out with the sword. Again they were moving in circles, the clash of their swords reverberating around the deck. Will was getting the upper

67

hand, Jack backed against the huge capstan wrapped around the base of the main mast.

He slashed wildly, making Will duck, and used the moment to jump up onto one of the capstan spokes and gain the upper ground. Will lunged the point of his sword at his stomach, making Jack lose his balance. As his arms flailed in the air in typical Jack Sparrow fashion, he managed to step back onto another spoke, and just about stay upright.

Will jumped up onto the spoke jack had just occupied, lashed out with his sword. But Jack had realised the mast could be his saving grace, and deftly moved to a third spoke. Now the mast was between them, and as they tried their best to swordfight as traditionally as they could, it was the mast that was getting most of it.

Each tried to lunge at the other, but the mast made it easy for both to avoid getting stabbed. But that wasn't the only thing they had to contend with.

As Will had jumped onto the capstan, he'd set it in motion. As they tried to fight each other and a thick mast as well, they were slowly rotating. And as they made each movement, it seemed to increase the speed of the capstan.

The guests were cheering and laughing at the antics of the two men, trying their hardest to kill each other while still keeping their balance on a merry-go-round. Daisy glanced to Aidan.

'Now I really can hear the music,' she grinned.

It got too much for the sparring partners. Like an out-of-control fairground ride, the capstan spat them both out. Jack sprinted to the quarterdeck steps, but didn't quite make it in time. Will got there first, and swung at him again. Once more the swords flew, the clash of sharpened steel filling the air.

As they fought, Jack managed to force Will to climb the steps slowly, one at a time. It didn't seem like either had an advantage, but just as Will reached the top step he let out an extra-hard slash, and Jack's sword clattered onto the deck below.

He looked at his empty hand in Sparrow-type horror, like he couldn't quite believe he'd been relieved of his weapon. For a full five seconds they looked into each other's eyes, neither of them moving a muscle.

It didn't make the sixth second. Jack reached into his tunic, pulled out a pistol. Will looked at the barrel pointing at him, shook his head in disbelief.

'You cheated.'

Jack shrugged, like it should have been expected. *'Pirate. Move away.'*

'No.'

'Please move?'

'No! I cannot just step aside and let you escape.'

Jack looked at the pistol, like shooting Will was the last thing he wanted to use the single shot for. Then again, what had to be, had to be. *'This shot is not meant for you...'*

He didn't get to fire. From the doorway to the Tortuga bar just next to the steps, Barbossa appeared, and smashed an imitation rum bottle over Jack's head.

A wide-eyed Jack crashed to the deck, unconscious, and Captain Barbossa lifted his arms from his sides to the guests. 'Well, me hearties, that was immensely satisfying!'

As Jack scrambled to his feet and he and Will took a bow, the appreciative crowd clapped and cheered. It was a fine and skilful exhibition after all, and very much in keeping with the spirit of the cruise.

Barbossa threw open the double doors to the Tortuga Bar. 'Now please come... enjoy the pirate fare we have prepared for you.'

The crew removed the temporary ropes, and the guests made their way into the quarterdeck bar. As Daisy, Aidan and Celia followed them, Daisy noticed someone hanging back, lurking next to the forecastle wall.

The wild dreadlocks, the black lips and the elaborate dress that had seen better days were all there, as was the black skin. She was clearly one of the guests, but she seemed to be alone, and didn't look like she was in any hurry to join the others.

'Look, Dip. That's Tia Dalma. She seems to be on her own... should we ask her to join us?'

He shook his head. 'I doubt she's alone. But she does look a bit furtive, I must say. And not terribly happy.'

As they watched, the woman turned away, climbed the steps to the forecastle roof, and disappeared. Daisy shook her head. 'Strange girl... for real I mean, as well as her character in the movies. Let's go eat, hey?'

They'd almost made the quarterdeck doors when Barbossa caught Aidan's arm. 'My friend, may we talk briefly, now?'

Daisy smiled to him. 'Go on, dear. Celia and me will find a table, and we'll see you in a few minutes, yes?'

He nodded, and followed the captain to the forward cabin. Daisy turned and looped an arm into Celia's. 'Guess it won't be too long until we find out why we're really here.'

She glanced back as they walked through the quarterdeck doors. Tia Dalma was nowhere to be seen, but she couldn't shake the uneasy feeling that noticing her had churned her stomach.

For some inexplicable reason, despite the dreds and the clever disguise of the costume, Daisy was convinced she'd seen her somewhere before.

Chapter 10

Ilya Komanichov's quarters were a little bigger than the others, and somewhat more opulent. And there was no cannon taking up part of the room. But there was a small oak desk, with a column of drawers each side of the kneehole.

He settled into the leather chair, indicated to his guest to sit in another chair on the far side of the desk, and pulled open a drawer. Aidan noticed a glass case fixed to the wall, with three ornate swords displayed in it.

'Those look valuable, and somewhat real.'

Ilya lifted out a bottle of vodka and two small glasses, and poured two shots, handed one to Aidan.

'To friendship... and cooperation,' he said in his heavy Russian accent, lifting his glass and downing the contents in one swig. 'Those swords are antiques, collected by myself when I first became fascinated by pirates. They are true eighteenth century, made by a master-craftsman... for real.'

'Then in one way, I guess they have come home.' Aidan took a sip of his vodka, frowned a question. 'Forgive me, Ilya, but we have not spoken for sixteen years, when we parted on less-than-friendly terms.'

'*Ush*... those days are gone, my friend. Now I think back, you were the one who was honest and forthright enough to expose my... shall we say, less-than-legal attempts to fool the UK taxman.'

'It was still down to me that those subterfuges were uncovered. Although it didn't hinder you very much, judging by what I read now.'

Ilya removed his captain's tricorn, dropped it onto the desk. 'It was a mere fly in the ointment, as you say. But let us allow bygones to be bygones, and look forward to new horizons, yes?'

'Now you sound like Barbossa.'

He laughed. 'Perhaps I am allowing my character a little too much leeway. But I confess, I am enjoying playing him, rather a lot.'

'Not exactly dissimilar to your true character, hey Ilya?'

His face clouded, but not with anger at Aidan's words. 'Perhaps, a few years ago. The good old days have gone, my friend. It became harder and harder to keep control, and my advancing years did not help. Whilst I yearn for the old simplicity of merely killing anyone who posed a threat to my family, in today's world it is not so possible without consequences.'

'A sign of the times, I suppose?'

Ilya poured another couple of shots. '*Ush*... do you know, I have not killed anyone for two years.'

'Shocking.'

He laughed again. 'In your world, that kind of flippant statement would sound like fantasy, I know. But in the world I moved in...'

'The Russian mafia, you mean.'

'Indeed. But we did not see ourselves as a cheap spin-off of Italian corruption. In Russia, everything was bigger, my friend.'

'You keep talking in past tense, Ilya.'

He shook his head, and a wave of sadness wafted across his whiskery features. 'Indeed I do. I am sure you know, in days gone by and since lost, I was the head of a feared family in Russia. But when my son was killed in a gang shooting in Moscow, I lost my appetite for looking over my shoulder every second of every day. These days my activities are more constrained, and more legal.' He waved

73

a hand in the air. 'This little venture, which is a passion of mine, is one example. My dalliance into oilfield exploration in the North Sea is another. In truth my friend, for a few years now my commercial activities have been wholly legitimate.'

'Paid for by your ill-gotten gains, of course.'

'You are no fool, my friend. Of course they were, but that is a symptom of today's world. The Black Pearl is perhaps symbolic of my regret for past demeanours, because although her operation should pay for itself, she will never show a profit.'

'So, is inviting us on this trip to say sorry too?'

'Not exactly.' Ilya reached into an inside breast pocket, pulled out a small leather pouch. 'I have a favour to ask of you, if you will make an old man happy and accept it.'

Aidan took the pouch, pulled open the strings, and lifted out the pendant. '*Oh I say*... a ruby of this size must be worth a fortune.'

'It is not a ruby, my friend. It is a red diamond, and worth even more of a fortune.'

Aidan turned it over in his hands. 'Yes, I can see that now. Forgive me my ignorance, Ilya. But what is it doing in my hand?'

The Russian looked like he didn't really want to ask the question he had to. 'I wish to beg of you to keep it hidden on your person, until we are safely at our destination in London.'

Aidan felt his heart start to thump in his ribcage. 'I think before I agree, you had better tell me the story.'

'Very well. That pendant is almost as old as the Black Pearl purports to be. It was made for a Russian Tsar, as a gift for his wife. Today, as an antique, and sporting one of the

74

biggest red diamonds in the world, it is worth several million pounds.'

'So it really is a pirate treasure to top all treasures.'

Ilya smiled ironically. 'Perhaps in more ways than you realise, my friend. When I acquired it...'

'Acquired?' said Aidan, narrowing his eyes.

Ilya poured another two shots, and then shook his head. 'When I acquired it from the Novalenko family, I thought no one would know it was me.'

'So you stole it?'

'It is the Russian way, my friend. The big families control everything, and no one gave a toss if one of them decided to possess a precious item once donated to the Moscow State Museum. It was almost inviting itself to be stolen, because whoever took it already knew the police would not dare to intervene.'

'That's a sad state of affairs.'

'Maybe so. I was already planning to steal it from the museum, but Novalenko got their first.'

Aidan was struggling to believe what he was hearing. 'So one crime family stole it from the museum, and then you stole it from them?'

'I had set my heart on it, as a gift for my daughter. She is now in her twenties, and due to be married in London next weekend. I wanted to give her something special as a wedding gift.'

'So you're a multi-millionaire, and you're giving your daughter something you *stole*?'

'As I said, my friend, it is...'

'Yes, I know. It's the Russian way.'

'I would not expect you to understand. But truth be told, I missed the old way of life. Going legitimate is somewhat...'

'Boring?'

75

'Indeed. Stealing the Crimson Heart from Novalenko was my last... fling, as it were. But unfortunately it has opened a can of worms, which is why I ask this favour of you now.'

The thumping in Aidan's ribcage wasn't going away. 'What kind of can of worms?' he asked cautiously.

Ilya sat back, shook his head in a frustrated kind of way. 'I had believed no one would be sure who had stolen it... the second time. It could have been any one of a dozen big Russian families. But somehow word got out, and I was informed the talk on the street was that I was the thief.'

'What goes around, Ilya.'

He nodded. 'I will admit something, Aidan, but it goes no further than these wooden walls, do you understand?'

'Do I really want to know?'

'Yes, I think you do. The truth is, I wish now I hadn't stolen it.'

'Then give it back.'

He threw both hands in the air. 'What, and disappoint my daughter on her wedding day?'

'Seriously?'

'It is not what you do in Russia, my friend. What is stolen stays stolen.'

Aidan shook his head. 'Yes I know, I wouldn't understand. You'd better tell me the rest.'

Ilya poured them a fourth shot of vodka. 'It came to my notice the Novalenko family were planning retribution, by stealing the Crimson Heart back from me. So I decided to attempt to fool them. I had a replica made, and took great pains to make sure everyone knew I was placing it in a vault at Barfly's bank for safe keeping until the wedding day. Of course, they stole it. But then I was told it had been revealed as a fake, and I actually did nothing but make them furious at my deception.'

'So I assume you kept the real one in your possession?'

'It has not left my side, until this moment.'

'So why now?'

He let out a deep sigh. 'Unfortunately, I have... what do you say... shot myself in the foot. Dimitri Novalenko is no fool, and considerably younger than me. I am certain he realises that in the circumstances I will not let it out of my sight. I personally selected the main personnel for this cruise, but there wasn't time to choose crewmen who have experience of sailing tall ships. That I had to leave to someone else, and it is not beyond the bounds of possibility the Novalenko family has got to them.'

'So you fear a mutiny, fuelled by the lure of the ultimate treasure.'

He nodded, and for a moment looked like a beaten man. 'Perhaps it is my Russian paranoia, my friend, but the possibility exists something may occur on this voyage, where we are ultimately on our own. I have... the jitters.'

'*You*... have the jitters?'

'As I said before, things are not what they were. I do not know who I can trust anymore... except for you.'

'And you believe you can trust me?'

'We are on a boat at sea, my friend. What can you possibly do to betray me?'

'I could still try.'

Ilya sank the last of his shot. 'If you do, then I will kill you. Nothing personal my friend, but it is...'

'Yes, I'm getting the picture. It's the Russian way.'

'I am glad we understand each other. So tell me please... can I rely on you?'

'I'm not sure you've given me much of a choice. But I won't be responsible for putting my family in danger, Ilya.'

He batted a dismissive hand in front of his face. 'Aidan, the reason I invited you along is that no one will suspect it is you carrying the Crimson Heart. A retired Brit accountant... who in their right mind would?'

Aidan ignored the slightly-offensive inference. 'So you don't think harm will come to any of us?'

'*Ush*... there is talk of a curse on anyone who possesses the pendant, but it is mere fantasy spread by illiterate Russian peasants. I am still here, am I not? You have nothing to worry about, my friend.'

Aidan nodded in a resigned way. 'So what do you want me to do?'

'Nothing. Enjoy the hospitality of the cruise. Keep the Crimson Heart hidden on your person at all times, including when you sleep tonight. When we disembark in London my daughter will be there to meet us, and to receive the pendant as her gift.'

'So what's to stop Novalenko stealing it from her?'

Ilya looked shocked. 'Do you know nothing about the Russian crime family code of honour?'

'*Code of Honour*?' said Aidan disbelievingly.

'Of course. Once a stolen item is given as a gift, it cannot be stolen again. That is why this voyage is the last chance for anyone to do so.'

'I see.'

'I doubt you do. But can I rely on your good nature, my friend?'

'I suppose so.'

Ilya poured them a final shot. 'Then we drink, to cooperation, and with disparaging mirth at ridiculous ancient curses!'

They drank together, one of them more enthusiastically than the other.

Aidan slipped away from Barbossa's quarters, headed to meet his family in the Tortuga bar, and sink a rum or two with more pleasant company. The thumping heart had subsided, but an uneasy feeling in his gut had replaced it. Daisy was right after all, and there was for sure a hidden reason they'd been invited.

A reason he couldn't really refuse to comply with; not if he wanted them all to walk away in one piece and never set eyes on Ilya Komanichov again. He was trapped by a smiling captor who called him his friend, but was quite prepared to see him as his enemy if he didn't do as he wished. He'd been deliberately shackled by invisible restraints, but ones he couldn't be freed from until he did what was being asked of him.

There was no choice, whichever way he looked at it.

Lost in his thoughts, he'd taken a quick glance around and not seen anyone on deck. But it was just a quick glance, and too brief for him to notice that someone actually was watching. Someone who had spotted him, and noted whose quarters he'd just left.

The black eyes followed Aidan as he disappeared from sight through the bar doors, and then their owner nodded knowingly, and slipped away.

Chapter 11

Daisy and Celia walked arm-in-arm into the quarterdeck bar. A timber-clad wall with a large square opening divided the space into two. Through the opening they could see the dining area, with its weathered wood tables spaced around the planked wooden floor, and the arched windows at the stern of the boat, offering an uninterrupted view of where they'd been.

On one side of the opening, two U-shaped seating areas with low tables had a few navy commanders and their elegantly-dressed wives, or *companions*, sitting enjoying drinks, obtained from the small bar built against the opposite wall.

Somewhere in the background, the accordion and fiddle music of sea shanties played through hidden speakers. Again, there was nothing visible to make them believe they hadn't time-travelled.

They headed to the bar, where a pirate sporting a green headscarf greeted them with a cheerful, gappy smile, two of his teeth blacked out.

'Arr, dear ladies. What can I be getting ye?'

Daisy grinned at the list of available drinks fixed to the wall behind his head with two daggers. There didn't seem to be a lot of choice...

Rum
Rum
Rum
Beer

'No pina colada then?'

'Why is rum listed three times?' Celia asked the pirate bartender.

'Arr well, you see... they's different rums. The first one bears a striking resemblance to the finest brandy; and the second one has a distinct flavour of barrelled malt whiskey.'

'And the third one?'

'That be rum, of course.'

'Of course.'

Daisy looked at her daughter. 'Two rums that taste like brandy then, Elizabeth?'

'A fine choice, my dear Anne.'

They walked through to the dining area, rums-that-taste-like-brandies in their hands, and found a table just in front of the latticed side windows. Standing on the tabletop was a short length of driftwood, with a piece of stiff parchment poked into a slot cut in it.

'Look, mum. It's the cruise itinerary.' Celia pulled the parchment out of the holder and read through the words written on it. 'It says we're heading for a quiet cove just inside the River Orwell estuary, which looks similar to Dead Man's Cove in Jamaica, where we'll drop anchor for the night. Then at first light we'll set off again, and arrive at the Port of London late afternoon.'

'Sounds good. I don't fancy getting tossed around in my hammock as we cruise the wild North Sea through the night.'

'Mum, it's almost flat calm.'

'Ah, but you know how these swells come out of nowhere.'

'And it's not a hammock, it's a memory-foam mattress.'

'You trying to spoil the ambience, Elizabeth?'

'No, I just don't want you getting lost in the game.'

'As if. So, how are you feeling so far?'

'Loving it. Jack and Will really knew what they were doing with those swords.'

'Yes dear, and Will is so dashing and handsome.'

'Mum...'

'I wonder where he lives?'

'*Mum*, please stop matchmaking.'

'Who, me?'

'Yes, you. I'm twenty-five; I can find my own companion... if and when I want to.'

'It sounds like you're not sure you want to?'

Celia's eyes turned a little misty. 'I'm damaged goods, mum. After the hell I've been through, who's going to want me?'

A stab of harsh reality speared into Daisy's heart. Her daughter had a point, but she knew all too well it was a hindrance, not a brick wall. She put a hand on Celia's arm. 'Hey you... if you find the *right* partner one day, none of that will matter. Look at your father and me. I was determined not to succumb to falling for someone, given what I did for a living, and yet...'

'You did save his life when you met. You could call that irresistibly romantic.'

'Maybe I saved a few people's lives that day. But I didn't fall in love with them all.'

'So why did you fall in love with dad?'

'It was that lock of hair that falls over his forehead.'

'*Seriously?*'

'Well, of course not. But after it was over and I went home, that was all I could think about.'

'Little things, huh?'

'Maybe. But that lock of hair was a symbol. A sign of what was to come.'

'And here I am.'

'Here you are... totally beautiful and amazing.'

'I suppose I look decent, on the outside. But inside It feels like I'm... broken.'

Daisy felt the stab again, tried not to show it. 'But not beyond repair. Having said that, your old mum and dad can only help fix so much. Someone else needs to step up and wield the tube of glue. And that Will is so dashing and handsome...'

'Mum...'

A waitress dressed in totally-impractical but authentic serving-wench dress came up to the table. 'Would ye ladies care to partake of some grub now?'

'What's on the menu?' asked Daisy.

'Smoked chicken with piquant and aromatic spices, served with rice and sweet potatoes, ma'am. Or, for them's who don't take meats, some kind of new-fangled concoction with nuts and lentils.'

'We'll take two chicken please.'

The waitress ambled away, wrote their order on a parchment scroll and placed it into a dumb waiter in the corner, then hauled on the ropes to wind it down to the kitchen on the floor below. Celia grinned to her mother.

'I guess jerk chicken had to surface somewhere!'

'I wonder if they'll give us some kind of spoon for the rice? Might be a little messy if they don't.'

'Now who's trying to diffuse the ambience?'

The stool next to them was pulled out from the table, and Aidan was there, a glass of rum-that-tasted-like-whiskey in his hands. He looked a little flustered, but greeted them with a smile. Daisy didn't look too impressed.

'Phew... you smell like a vodka distillery.'

'Sorry. Ilya would insist on us drinking a toast or two.'

'To what?'

'Oh, you know... the good old days and all that.'

'So that was all he wanted?'

'Well, he's left his illegal ways behind him. Totally legit now.'

'And you fell for that?'

He threw Daisy an expression she'd only ever seen once before, spoke a little curtly. 'Why do you insist on thinking there's something untoward going on, hey?'

Daisy sat back, a little shocked by his tone. 'Ok, dear. Don't get your pink pantaloons in a twist. We've just ordered jerk chicken. Shall I ask for a third portion, or are you going to go off and sulk?'

He forced a smile. 'Sorry. It's not your fault. Let's just enjoy the afternoon, yes?'

Daisy narrowed her eyes. 'Whatever you say, dear.'

Chapter 12

As the afternoon turned into early evening and the sun began to sink over the low hills of Suffolk, the Black Pearl made its way into the Orwell estuary.

Daisy and Aidan had spent much of the time on deck, soaking in the atmosphere, the billowing black sails and the sounds of a pirate ship propelled by just the wind making them believe they really had stepped back in time.

Daisy had gently pumped Aidan for the real reasons behind his meeting with Barbossa, but he'd grown a little short with her again, so she'd decided pumping was a bad idea. Convinced there was more to it than meets the eye, she was forced to accept that whatever it was, he wasn't going to give.

As the ship reached the cove, there was a flurry of activity from the sailing crew. The sails were furled, and as they came to a virtual stop a quarter-mile from the wooded shore, the evocative sounds of the anchor dropping filled their ears.

They'd reached their overnight stop, and suddenly all was at peace.

Daisy clicked away on her phone, taking pictures of the sheltered bay and the sunset, and sending them to Sarah as promised. Their friend called back briefly, mainly to say how envious she was, and how much she wished she'd gone AWOL after all.

Then, as the sun finally disappeared, and a few stars began to appear in the darkening sky, Daisy let out a shiver. 'I think we should go find some grub, Dip. Get in the warm. Time to leave the chill of the night to the younger ones.'

He nodded his agreement, and they made their way across the deck towards the Tortuga bar doors. They were the last ones topsides... but not quite. As Daisy cast her eyes around for a final time, she noticed a dark figure lurking silently in the shadows of the quarterdeck.

The mysterious Tia Dalma was standing there, unmoving, watching them. Daisy narrowed her eyes to see her better, and once again got the feeling she'd seen her somewhere before. Trying to look beyond the wild dreadlocks and the clever makeup, she didn't really get long enough. Aidan had his arm around her waist, steering her through the bar doors, and not really giving her a chance to study her features.

Yet once again the Jamaican sorceress seemed to be alone, a solitary figure who was giving Daisy the uneasy feeling they were being deliberately watched. Rather like her character in the movies, she was doing a very good job of spooking her out.

As they ate a meal of curried beef, that according to the serving wench was goat's meat, accompanied by rice, and ships biscuits that tasted a lot like peshwari naans.

Celia couldn't help remarking on the lack of conversation. 'You two are quiet tonight. Have I done something wrong, or are you just in a strop with each other?'

Her parents both protested together. 'Of course not, dear. We're fine.'

'You're not fine. You look troubled, dad. And you mum, you seem like you're somewhere else. Is there something I should know about?'

Aidan still wasn't giving. 'It's been a tiring day, Celia. Us wrinklies, we can't take the rigours of being transported back in time like we used to, you know. I think I shall hit the hammock before too long.'

'Don't give me that. Mum?'

'If you must know, I was thinking about someone.'

'Ah, now you're getting interesting. If you don't want to talk about it in front of dad, I will understand,' Celia grinned.

'Glad to see you've not lost your sense of humour. Actually, I was thinking about Tia Dalma. Have you seen her?'

'I spotted her just after we left Great Yarmouth. Top costume. But I've not noticed her since.'

'Your mother thinks she's seen her somewhere before,' said Aidan.

'Mum... you never told me you appeared in the POTC movies!'

'No, not that. I just get the feeling I've seen the woman behind the costume before. I'm trying to go back in my mind to when and where it might have been.'

Celia glanced to her father, who narrowed his eyes at his wife. 'What... no witty retort, Flower?'

'Sorry. I think I really am somewhere else.'

She went back to absent-mindedly chewing a piece of curried beef, and said no more. Celia shook her head, a little dejectedly. 'I do so enjoy these scintillating conversations we have over dinner.'

Aidan looked a little apologetic, tried to make conversation. 'They chose a beautiful spot here... if you ignore the very distant sight of container ships heading in and out of the Port of Felixstowe, we actually could be in the Caribbean.'

He didn't get any further. A shout from Daisy almost forced him to drop his wooden spoon, and made a few other diners look round.

'I've got it!'

'Got what?'

Daisy lowered her voice, leant over the table with a triumphant smile. 'I know who she is.'

'Naomie Harris?' grinned Celia.

'Funny girl. But she's even more scary than Tia Dalma.'

'Are you going to tell us her name?'

'Irina Novichokopopolov.'

'Irina Novi... *what?'*

'You might find it easier to get your chops around her nickname.'

Celia shook her head. 'She's got a nick? This must be serious.'

'Indeed... for someone, anyway.'

'Please tell us, so I don't have to try pronouncing her name ever again.'

'She's known as the Black Russian.'

'Isn't that a cocktail?'

'Not if you're a member of the Russian mafia, no.'

'The...'

'Yes dear. If the Black Russian is on board, then we've got trouble.'

Aidan swallowed hard, tried not to let it show he had. 'I suppose I don't need to ask how you are aware of all this, dear?'

'Not really. When I retired from active field duty twenty-odd years ago, as you know I went into central surveillance, as a desk-based operative whose job was to discover and watch people who might be a potential threat to international security. A year before I fully retired, one of the people I flagged was Irina. She was sixteen at the time.'

'Sixteen?'

'Yes. The daughter of a Jamaican mother and a Russian father, he was killed as an innocent bystander in a gang family shootout in Chechnya. He and his daughter were extremely close. She took his death badly.'

'It must have been pretty badly, if MI6 got involved?'

'After she mourned him, she swore to devote her life to doing everything she could to make things as difficult as possible for the Russian mafia families. And somehow she survived that pledge, and over the years grew to be feared and respected. She's like a ghost, appears from nowhere, leaves her mark, and then disappears again before the bad guys can catch her. I'm quite surprised she's still alive.'

'Go her, I say.'

'She's been linked to a number of assassinations, and countless other activities, but there has never been solid proof she's actually done anything wrong. Although 'wrong' is a debatable point.'

'Are you sure Tia Dalma is her?'

'Yes. I've never actually met her, just seen a lot of photos. But unfortunately for us, there has to be a reason she's here, and right now I haven't a clue what that reason is. I don't suppose either of you have any idea?'

Celia shook her head.

'Not a clue,' said Aidan quietly.

Chapter 13

Celia felt a little restless. It was almost eleven in the evening, but somehow she knew sleep wasn't going to come easily. Her parents had retired to their adjacent cabin a while back, and she hoped they had found sleep, although that too was by no means a certainty.

At dinner, both of them had looked like they had the weight of the world on their shoulders, and it wasn't sitting easily with their daughter. Her mother's unease was clear enough; finally working out who Tia Dalma was had led to her spending the rest of the meal wondering why she was there, and not exactly being satisfied with the question she couldn't answer right then.

But her father was a different kettle of fish. He'd always worn his heart on his sleeve, and as far as she knew, never kept anything from her. Back in the awful few months before she'd been taken, he was the one who told it like it was, when her mother was succumbing to the emotional pressure of a daughter who refused to see the downward spiral she was locked into.

He was the sensible one, the one who kept his girls as grounded as he could. Yet that evening he'd been defensive and withdrawn. Something had happened, but he wasn't giving anything away.

And that wasn't like him.

She reached behind her and began to unzip the beautiful dress ready for bed, but then hesitated. Sleep wasn't going to come, not without breaking her thought pattern first. She zipped it up again, deciding a little fresh, chilly air might help. There was unlikely to be anyone else on deck, so a little solo star-gazing might be just what she needed.

She slipped out of her cabin, climbed the staircase, and stepped onto the deck. She was right, there was no one there. Then, as she cast her eyes around, she realised she was wrong. Someone *was* there, up on the quarterdeck, gazing out to sea with his arms resting on the deck rail, looking like he was deep in thought.

'A beautiful night, Mr. Turner.'

He looked round, a little startled that someone was standing next to him. 'Miss Swann,' he said, a slight smile creasing his face, for a second making him look just like Orlando Bloom.

'Please, call me Elizabeth.'

He turned to gaze back across the water. 'It is a lovely night, made even more beautiful by your presence.'

'You are too kind.'

'No... I speak with truth. The dress you wear so perfectly is but a compliment to the rest of you.' He lowered his eyes, looked embarrassed. 'But I speak out of turn.'

'You do not. Perhaps I may appreciate receiving compliments from someone who is not a member of my family.'

'Then I should regale you with more.'

'As you wish. But I must return your good words. Your prowess with a sword today was most impressive.'

He turned back to her, grinned. 'Well, I am the son of a blacksmith.'

'You do yourself down, Mr. Turner. That alone does not make you a fine swordsman.'

'Perhaps, but a few weeks of practice makes me an acceptable one.'

'And there was I under the assumption you had practiced three hours a day for many years.'

He laughed. 'I see my lines made an impression on you, Elizabeth.'

'Not just your lines, Will. Your athletic abilities did not go unnoticed.'

He nodded. 'I am truly flattered.' Then he shook his head a little, held out a hand. 'Forgive me. I'm Jack.'

'Now I'm confused.'

He chuckled. 'No, I mean in real life. My name is actually Jack, ironically.'

She took his hand, held on to it a moment longer than she needed to. 'I'm Celia. Pleased to meet you.'

'Believe me, it is my pleasure.'

He turned back to the rail, leant his arms on it again, and for a moment a wave of sadness wafted across his features. Celia did the same, and then turned her head to look at him.

'Can I offer you something, Jack?'

'If you wish.'

'I want to offer you a piece of eight for your thoughts.'

'I'm sorry?'

She laughed. 'Well, I would offer you a penny for them, but a piece of eight sounded more appropriate. You were lost in something when I walked up to you, and you didn't even realise I was there until I spoke. Are you missing your girl, or someone?'

He wouldn't look at her. 'No, nothing like that. There's no one else, not right now.'

'You don't have to tell me anything. I am a total stranger after all.'

Finally he turned and smiled. 'I thought we first met when we were children? I seem to remember you saving my life.'

Celia smiled too, recalling the opening scene of the first movie. 'That was then, this is now. But I still want to know what matters to the grown-up you... if you want to tell me, of course.'

He shook his head, but then seemed to change his mind. 'I could never keep anything from you. I was just musing over what I've got myself into.'

'I'm not quite sure what you mean.'

'I don't expect you to understand. A lady of your standing has no perception of what it's like to be a poor... pirate.'

Celia lowered her head. 'Don't be fooled by what you see, Jack. This lady of standing has a past that is less than unblemished.'

He stood up straight, a little shocked by her words. 'Why Elizabeth... how could someone so beautiful say such things? Sorry, I keep slipping back into character.'

'It's ok. Kind of cute really. But I have to be honest with you, seeing as you've been in love with me all these years.'

He laughed, a little nervously. Celia knew she was pouring out her heart to a total stranger, but somehow it felt like the right thing to do. 'I've just come out of a detox clinic, after being imprisoned by an evil African general for three years, who drugged me every day to keep me submissive. But even before all that happened I'd... succumbed to hard drugs, and wasn't prepared to admit I had a problem.'

His eyes widened. '*Oh my god*... all that shit happened, and still you look like *that*?'

Celia felt herself blushing, but for some strange reason it was a nice feeling. 'You should have seen me three weeks ago.'

He reached out, took her hand, spoke almost in a whisper. 'You have taken the breath from my lungs. What you went through would have spelled the end for most women. Yet now... *look at you...*'

She didn't let go of his hand. She didn't want to. 'As Elizabeth would say, you're too kind.'

'Oh no... a little awestruck perhaps. I look into your eyes, and there I see true beauty. The kind that can only come from strong spirit. I am humbled by your inner strength. Perhaps you truly are Elizabeth Swann.'

'If I am, then for sure you are the man I genuinely love.'

His head lowered, he let go of her hand and turned away. 'Then rather like the movie, we are from different sides of the bay. You would be well advised to steer clear of me.'

She spun him round to face her. 'And you, Will, would be well advised to not let go of my hand. Are you hearing me?'

She watched as his arm hesitantly left his side, and then their hands curled slowly together. He shook his head, like he couldn't quite believe what he was doing. 'This is a little freaky.'

'So we mix fantasy with reality. Whatever is going on here, it feels like I want to be in its spell.'

They were two feet away from each other, unable to break away, unable to move closer. For a full minute their gazes locked together, neither of them wishing to do something that might dispel the magic.

Then, for Celia, doing nothing got too much. Almost without knowing what her body was doing, it threw itself at Will, and their lips blended together into a perfect, passionate kiss. It seemed to last a whole scene, but then he broke away, a nervous, shocked smile quivering over his face.

94

Celia took a step back, equally stunned by what had just happened. 'So then, was that fantasy or reality?' she gasped.

He looked up to the myriad of stars above their heads, breathed out the words. 'It might have been fantasy, but it sure felt as real as hell.'

'Then, Mr. Turner, you have something else to occupy your thoughts.'

He nodded, almost reluctantly. 'Fantasy is one thing, but by the cold light of morning it will all be harsh reality.'

His words unsettled her. 'Perhaps it is up to us to decide that, Will?'

'How I wish, Elizabeth. Sadly for us, circumstances will decide our fate.'

He backed away a few steps. Celia suddenly felt the cold air of the gulf between them, which wasn't just a very real ten feet. 'Tell me what you mean by that, please..?'

He shook his head, turned and began to walk away, but then glanced back. 'I will protect you Elizabeth, please be assured of that...'

'Will...'

He was gone, disappearing into the shadows like a ghost. Celia lifted her arms from her sides, a gesture that betrayed the frustration she was feeling. He was saying things she couldn't understand. For a moment she started to follow him, but then checked herself up.

Rather like some other people on the ship, she knew he wasn't going to give any more.

She headed back to her cabin, unzipped the dress and slumped down on the elegant bed. She'd intended the stroll on the deck to help clear her mind, get her ready for sleep.

Instead she'd been presented with a whole new scenario, which was for sure all too real.

She pulled the thick duvet over herself, knowing sleep was even less likely to come. Her thoughts flashed lightning bolts behind the eyelids she tried to keep closed, and rather like the previous hour, they seemed to be a blend of fantasy and real life. Perhaps in another existence she *had* saved Will's life when he was a boy. Perhaps somehow destiny was meant to play out like the plot in a movie.

But none of that seemed to matter as much as the taste of his kiss, which was certain to stay on her lips for the whole night, and beyond.

Chapter 14

Aidan seemed to be afflicted by the same curse as his daughter. As the clock ticked to one in the morning, he still hadn't found sleep. And like Celia, he reluctantly decided a little cold night air might solve the problem.

He slipped his gown over the full-length pyjamas he'd packed instead of the long nightgown Calico Jack would likely have worn, and headed for the deck. Like Celia, he thought he was alone. Unlike his daughter, for five minutes he *was* alone, leaning his arms on the deck rail as Will had done, and doing his best to mesmerise himself to sleep mode by watching the moonlight glinting off the gently-moving water.

Then he got the strange feeling someone else was there. It wasn't a wrong feeling. She seemed to appear from nowhere, sidling up to his side almost like she was on wheels.

'Him give you trouble in yur thoughts, Calico?' she said in a thick old-Jamaican accent.

Startled, he looked at the woman, still clothed in the long dress of autumn colours, with the beads of mystic power around her neck. 'Who him... he... who do you mean?' he stammered.

'Captain Barbossa. Dat who him.'

'I don't know what you mean.'

'Me tinks you do.'

'I... I'm just a retired accountant, Tia,' he stammered again.

She moved up close to him, smiled to show her vegetable-dye-blackened teeth, and tapped him on the

97

nose with a forefinger. 'If ye know me name, then ye know I know tings mere mortals do not.'

'I... know... do I?'

She leant her slim forearms on the deck rail, gazed across the bay as she spoke. 'Ye cannot fight the power of the curse, Calico. Him already cursed, and ye are next.'

'Who him? I mean... who is cursed?'

'Me already tell you. Captain Barbossa.'

'Oh come on, Tia. That's just Disney movie fantasy.'

She turned, fixed her dark eyes into his. 'And ye are sure of dat?'

'I... of course I am.'

'So him did not tell ye of the curse of the Crimson Heart?'

'Him... *he* might have mentioned it, in a dismissive kind of way.'

She shook her head slowly from side to side. 'Then him foolish man. Me do not see ye as so foolish.'

Aidan, getting his brain back in gear from the shock of a mysterious voodoo sorceress standing next to him, found his confidence flooding back too. 'I know who you are, you know.'

'Of course ye do. Me is Tia Dalma... or Calypso, if ye like.'

'No you're not. You're Irina Novicho... the Black Russian.'

The accent changed, to a considerably more Russian one. '*Ush*... I knew you were not so foolish. And not what you seem.'

'You can talk.'

'It was necessary to get on board.'

'Why? What could you possibly do on a pirate ship out at sea?'

She turned to look at him, answered a question with one of her own. 'So how does a retired accountant know who I am?'

'In truth, I didn't. My wife recognised you.'

'So she is Russian mafia too?'

'Good god no. But she used to be with MI6, and they were observing you.'

'*Ush*... interfering busybodies.'

'From what she tells me, they were actually leaving you to your... activities.'

'I do not believe you. There is more to you than meets the eye, Calico Jack.'

'That's up to you. But I'm no threat to whatever it is you plan to do.'

She turned away again, shook her head like she really didn't believe him. 'So why you have the Crimson Heart then?'

'I... I didn't say I had.'

'But you are not surprised I asked that question?'

'No, Barbossa... Ilya told me about it.'

'So it is here somewhere?'

'I didn't say that either.'

The accent switched again, as she put her head close to his once more. 'Metinks you did.'

'Think what you like, Irina.'

'*Ush*... you are difficult man to crack, Calico. I admire that in a man.'

'I shall take that as a compliment.'

She walked away a few steps. 'You are still a foolish one though. The curse does its worst to whoever possesses the Crimson Heart... even those who only do so temporarily.'

'You're just trying to scare me.'

'Do I succeed, Calico Jack Rackham?'

'Not in the slightest.'

'Then you are even more foolish than I thought. The pendant belongs to the state, not... however many Russian mafia families.'

'Is that why you're here? To steal it back?'

She let out a scary laugh. '*Steal it?* I cannot steal something that does not belong to those who actually did steal it.'

Aidan shook his head. 'You make a good point.'

She moved back to him, pressed her body up against his. 'Then give it to me, before the curse devours you.'

'I... I can't. And please stop with the curse nonsense.'

She turned, began to walk away. 'So you want it for yourself?'

'I didn't say that. That's not what I meant.'

Tia Dalma was back. 'Be it on yur head, Calico. And brace yeself, 'cos dat curse will strike, without warning. And those who laugh at its power will suffer, be sure of dat.'

Aidan shook his head, more to convince himself it was all nonsense than anything else, and leant back on the deck rail. Ten seconds later he turned to say something, but the words never came.

Tia Dalma was gone. Like she'd never been there at all.

Aidan let out a huge shiver, unsure if it was the cold of the night or the things he'd been told. He wrapped his long coat tighter around him, and headed back to the warmth of the cabin.

Daisy was still spark out, luckily. Talking with her or anyone else was the last thing he wanted to do right then. He slipped gently into bed beside her, and lay on his back for a while, forcing his heart rate down to a safe level.

Like his daughter an hour earlier, a quiet solo stroll on the deck hadn't exactly turned out the way he'd expected. And hadn't exactly settled his mind like it was supposed to.

Sleep felt like it was a million miles away. But after a while, those miles dwindled to nothing, helped by a strange kind of exhaustion that welled over him and took away the disturbing thoughts that flicked from fantasy to reality.

But as he finally fell asleep, he just had time to make a decision. In the morning he would give the Crimson Heart back to Ilya Komanichov, and hang the consequences.

It was one step better to face his wrath than the ravages of an ancient curse, which he'd already admitted to himself could be either fantasy or harsh reality.

Chapter 15

Aidan woke suddenly. Despite his near-panic, he'd fallen into a deep sleep, and it took a moment to remember where he was. As reality slowly replaced unconsciousness he forced bleary eyes to open, and realised daylight was streaming through the gun-port window.

Then he noticed he was alone under the duvet, turned on his back, and saw Daisy sitting on the end of the bed, fixing one of her glares into him. As his vision cleared, he gasped in shock at what he saw, which had the instant effect of wrenching him fully awake in a single second.

'About time you woke up,' she said, not exactly sounding friendly.

'What...'

'Sorry I spoilt the surprise... but it is lovely. Thank you so much, darling.'

'I...' As he sat up with his heart pounding, still unable to form a single sentence, Daisy lifted the Crimson Heart from around her neck, and gazed lovingly at it. *'So beautiful...'*

'You found it then,' he whispered, finally able to put more than one word together.

'Well dear, when you roll over and half-crush me in the night, and I ease you back over and feel a nasty lump in your pyjama pocket, I get a little worried,' she replied sarcastically.

'I suppose you want to know how it got there?'

'Not at all, dear. I'm just so thrilled you bought it for me.'

'I... I could never afford that, Flower,' he said sheepishly.

'You don't say.'

'Ok, you've rumbled me. So just stop glaring at me like that, and I'll tell you the truth.'

'Only if you *really* want to, my darling.'

'Please, give it a rest now.'

Aidan confessed all, which did little to stop the glare. It did change the emotions behind it though, which switched from suspicion to fear. As he told her every gruesome detail, Daisy felt her heart begin to thump in her chest, which then decided to bounce around her ribcage with increasing speed. Whichever way she came at it, their situation was even more perilous than it pretended to be.

'I told you.'

'Yes dear... I should listen to your superior gut.'

'Now *you're* being sarcastic. Just remember, you're in no position to be sarky.'

His head lowered. 'Sorry, Flower.'

She handed the pendant back to him, and then gave him a hug. 'From what I'm seeing none of it was your doing, and I do understand your reasons for not telling me.'

'Thank you.'

'You still should have spilled your guts though.'

'Perhaps not the best choice of expression, dear.'

Daisy walked over to the cannon, looked out of the gun-port window. 'Sorry. Guess I'm lost in the game a bit. So how do we stop from being hung, drawn and quartered now?'

'Please stop it.'

'Ok, *I'm* sorry now. Just my wicked side.'

'I'm going to give Ilya back the pendant this morning, tell him I don't want anything to do with it.'

'So how will that stop us getting hung, dr... sorry, getting killed?'

'I don't know. I doubt he would actually end our lives. He just said that to put the fear of god into me.'

'Are you sure about that?'

'Don't you start. My cosy chat with the voodoo sorceress last night made me question my convictions.'

'Maybe she's right.'

'Please don't tell me that's your gut speaking again?'

'No. It's quiet right now, apart from a little nervous gurgling. Just a throwaway comment.'

'I don't have any truck with ancient curses... I don't think.'

'Please try and sound more convincing, dear.'

'I wish I could.'

Daisy walked back over to the bed, slipped under the duvet and took Aidan's hand. He could feel hers shaking a little as he smiled unconvincingly to her. 'I'll do everything I can to put this right. Please just believe it seemed like I had no choice.'

She laid her head onto his chest. 'I do believe that, dear. Impossible situation and everything. But whatever we do next, we're in a volatile scenario here, with no escape other than swimming to the shore. Ilya clearly believes something might happen, and from what you tell me, he's very likely right. Whatever we do, we've got to have eyes in the back of our head.'

Aidan was about to agree, but didn't get the chance. The door burst open, and a breathless and wide-eyed Celia stood there, grasping the doorframe for support. *'Guys... something dreadful has happened...'*

'Celia..?' Daisy was out of bed in an instant, with Aidan close behind. 'What's the matter?'

'You'd better come up on deck and see,' she sobbed.

They dressed quickly and ran after their daughter, up the short staircase and onto the main deck, where a small group of shell-shocked guests were standing motionless, staring silently into the air.

Daisy and Aidan followed their eyes, and Aidan passed a terrified hand across his mouth. Daisy slipped a hand into his free one.

'So now do you believe in ancient curses, dear?'

Chapter 16

Nobody seemed able to say anything, too dumbfounded to utter a word. Captain Barbossa definitely wasn't able to speak.

Hanging from a rope around his neck forty feet above their heads, he was very, very dead.

Daisy glanced to Aidan, and saw the terrified fear in his eyes, which undoubtedly matched her own. 'In all my days, I've never seen anyone hung from the yardarm before, dear,' she whispered.

Celia let out a sob, and Daisy pulled her tight, thrust her head into her shoulder to try and tear her eyes away from the gruesome sight. She couldn't tear her own eyes away from it though, or her mind away from the implications of the fact a dead body was swinging in the slight breeze halfway up the main mast, and it sure hadn't got there by accident.

Jack Sparrow came running from the forecastle cabin, stopped dead when he saw what everyone else was staring at. 'Well, that wasn't supposed to happen,' he said flatly.

Celia glared at him. 'Is that all you can say, Jack Sparrow? The captain is dead, and someone has committed murder on a ship you call your own?'

He looked a little taken aback by her hysteria. 'I can assure you, dear lady, we might have had our differences as to the rightful captaincy of said vessel, but it wasn't me who put him there.'

'*Oohh*...' Celia turned away, buried her face back in her mother's shoulder. Daisy glanced to Aidan again. 'How the hell did he get up there anyway?'

'I don't know, but it's a little unnerving. We can't leave him there though.'

'Will somebody do something?' said a voice from the crowd.

Daisy pulled her phone from her breeches pocket. 'We have to call the police... *oh...'*

Aidan looked over her shoulder. 'No signal, dear?'

'Not a single bar. It's strange, I talked to Sarah just after we got here last night.'

Someone in the crowd confirmed her growing suspicions. 'My phone is dead too.'

'And mine,' someone else said hesitantly.

'Looks like we're all at sea, dears,' Daisy whispered.

'What's going on?' a frantic woman's voice cried out.

Then someone else appeared, pushing through the crowd, most of whom seemed to want to steer clear of him as soon as they saw him. Daisy and Aidan hadn't set eyes on him before. A tattered tricorn topped his gruesome head, most of which was covered by a full blue-green prosthetic mask. It seemed to have a life of its own, a mass of writhing tentacles making up what should have been his hair, his beard, and even some of his face.

'Davy Jones?' Daisy gasped. 'Where did he come from?'

'Somewhere under the sea?' said Aidan.

Daisy gave him the glare. 'I meant, we've not seen him before. Whoever he is, he's kept himself shut away until now. And that prosthetic must have cost a fortune.'

'Yes, but what a disguise if you don't want anyone to know who you are.'

Davy Jones glanced up to the body hanging above his head. 'An unfortunate development, for sure. But it does not alter the fact this ship is now under my control.'

107

Jack didn't seem to think too much of that. 'Um... excuse me, tentacle face, but pray tell, who actually made you captain of this vessel?'

Davy Jones drew his sword, stuck the tip under Jack's chin, and rasped out the words. 'So, you little ship's rat, do we have a problem with that?'

'Well, in fairness, the problem is not the problem. Your attitude to the problem seems to be the problem,' he muttered, still being Jack.

'Oh really? So you have a problem with my attitude to the problem?'

'In all honesty, the problem with your attitude to the problem might end up being a problem.'

The point of the sword made a slight dent in Jack's chin. 'It seems to me Jack, the only problem to my attitude to the problem is *your* attitude to the problem.'

'Um... it might just be that there are so many problems emerging here that I may have become somewhat confused as to what the original problem was.'

Someone in the crowd shouted out, in a hopeful kind of way. 'Oh, I get it... it's another re-enactment.'

Davy Jones didn't seem to appreciate that much. He spun away from Jack, and sliced his sword into the rope keeping Captain Barbossa hanging from the yardarm. The body headed rapidly downwards, and hit the main deck with a sickening thud.

'Does this look like a re-enactment to you, fool?'

It didn't look like a re-enactment. There weren't usually dead bodies in role play.

Daisy had seen enough death in her previous life, but this time her family had witnessed it too. Something snapped inside her. She drew her sword, and stood six feet

108

away from the man of the sea with her legs apart, like all the most fearsome female pirates do.

'*Daisy...*' Aidan groaned. 'That's just a pretend sword... isn't it?'

She ignored him, snarled out the words to her opponent instead. 'You think we're just going to roll over and let you do your worst, Mr. Jones?'

He laughed disparagingly, braced his sword threateningly. 'So, Miss Bonny, you think you and your fake sword can get the better of me?'

'Try me.'

Several members of the crew had gathered behind Davy Jones. They also drew their swords, but he waved them to back down. 'Leave it be, men. This pathetic bilge rat is all mine...'

He grinned confidently through the tentacles, took off his tattered tricorn and threw it to the ground. 'Show me what you possess, wench,' he growled.

Daisy raised her sword, matched his menacing glare. But then he shook his head. *'Wait.'*

'*What?* Death waits for no man, Davy Jones. Even if you are already dead.'

'Just... give me a few seconds. This mask is driving me crazy.'

He fumbled with the prosthetic, finally managing to rip it from his head, and threw it to the deck between him and Daisy.

'*Dimitri...*' someone in the crowd gasped their recognition.

Celia looked at the mask in horror. '*Eeuw*... it's still writhing.'

Daisy glanced down to the tentacled prosthetic. It *was* still wriggling slowly, like some kind of alien entity unable to

109

escape. She shook her head in a disgusted kind of way, and then raised her sword with both hands, and stabbed it so hard the point buried itself in the plank underneath it.

It let out a strange kind of strangled final gasp, and a tiny wisp of smoke curled upwards as the electronic wizardry writhed its last breath.

'Now it's not irritating anybody. Unlike you, Mr. Jones.'

Aidan nodded his head in realisation. 'That sword *isn't* fake. I might have known...'

Davy Jones saw Daisy's sword was buried in the deck, and knew that for a second or two he might have the upper hand. He lunged at Daisy, but she ducked and managed to prise the sword from the deck plank.

The sword was free of the deck, but not from the gruesome mask. Speared onto the blade like a marshmallow on a toasting fork, Daisy swung the sword viciously in Davy Jones's direction. The inertia freed the mask, which flew in the general direction of its owner, slapping him in the face it had been ripped away from a minute earlier.

Daisy followed the trajectory of the mask, in a single second thrusting the sword against her opponent's neck. As he brushed the dead tentacles away, he met her crazed stare with shock and disbelief.

'*Seriously?* You defeated me with my own mask?'

Lost in the game that wasn't a game at all, Daisy tightened her grip on the hilt, and growled out the words. 'Prepare to die, again, Davy Jones...'

'*Enough!*'

Chapter 17

'Much as it goes against the grain to mention this, I am of the considered opinion one dead body per day is enough for any pirate, do you not think?'

'So can I kill him tomorrow then?'

Jack speared the dead mask off the deck with the tip of his sword, and dropped it over the side. 'Let's send that back where it belongs, shall we?'

Aidan grasped his still-protesting wife by the arms. 'Dear, we should address the real problem, shouldn't we?'

'Don't you start with *problems*,' she glared back, but allowed herself to be dragged away from the fight.

Davy Jones was recovering his composure, helped by the mutineering crewmen. He called out to the watching crowd, in an accent that was less Davy Jones, more Vladimir Putin.

'Listen up, all of you. The Black Pearl is now under my control. Do not try to contact anyone; we have activated a communications blocker, so none of your devices will transmit or receive a signal. We are on our own, and no one is coming to help you. But you can help yourselves. Do as we tell you, and none of you will be harmed.'

'Are you listening to this, dear?' Aidan asked Daisy in a small, hesitant voice.

'Of course, Dip,' she said, without meeting his gaze.

'In a few minutes we shall be setting sail as planned, but travelling to a destination I have no intention of revealing to you. For now you will return to your cabins, and remain there until instructed otherwise. My men will visit each of your quarters, where you, your belongings and your accommodation will be thoroughly and completely searched. Do not resist them, and do not try anything futile, or you will discover just how unpleasant mutineers on a pirate ship can be. Do I speak clearly?'

A murmur of frightened acknowledgement drifted from the crowd.

'Good. Now do as you have been instructed, and let us get this matter resolved as quickly as possible.'

The crowd began to scuttle back down the stairs to their cabins. 'I wonder what they're searching for?' asked Aidan.

'Treasure, as you well know,' said Daisy sarcastically.

'What do I do?' he let out a panic-stricken whisper.

'Nothing, not right now. Let's get on our own, and then we'll plan what to do next.'

'What to do next? We're alone on a pirate ship in the North Sea with the Russian mafia for company, we're all effectively hostages of modern-day pirates who don't really give a toss about human life, and no one on land has a clue there's anything wrong. I think our options are somewhat limited, dear.'

'I've still got a sword.'

'Yes, and that's something else I need to discuss with you.'

'I couldn't exactly bring my automatic rifle, could I? And I did kill the prosthetic, after all.'

'Indeed, and if Jack Sparrow hadn't stopped you, you'd probably have killed its owner too, come what may.'

'Dear, you're exaggerating... I think.'

He shook his head, and they turned to follow the other guests down the stairs. Then Daisy realised their daughter wasn't with them, and glanced back. Celia was standing motionless on the deck, her eyes raised to the upper quarterdeck. Daisy followed her gaze, to where Will Turner was just hitching his sword into its scabbard, and helping the other mutineers hoist the sails.

112

He must have felt her silent stare boring into him, stopped what he was doing and looked back to her, a pained, regretful expression on his face. He lifted his arms from his sides in a resigned kind of way, and then shook his head sadly, and almost imperceptibly.

Then someone shouted for a hand, and he turned away and grabbed a rope.

Daisy slipped an arm around her daughter's waist, felt her body trembling, and realised straightaway what the silent exchange of emotion was all about. The tears of betrayal in her daughter's eyes just confirmed how she was feeling.

Daisy eased her away, already knowing the next few hours would be tough for her daughter. There were no words of consolation she could utter, so instead she verbally chastised herself.

'Sadly, I can't be right about everything, dear. But there are times when I really wish I was.'

Chapter 18

Aidan slumped onto the four-poster bed, his stomach churning. He was alone, Daisy spending a little time with Celia in her cabin to try and console her.

He didn't know what to do. Intending to give back the Crimson Heart to Ilya and washing his hands of the whole thing, that was no longer an option.

You can't give something back to someone who has been murdered.

The reason he'd lost his life wasn't difficult to work out. Sometime in the night Davy Jones had risen from the sea, intent on getting back what he believed was his. Confronting Barbossa, who had held his ground and refused to give it up, he'd ended up getting hung from the yardarm for his defiance.

But was Davy Jones actually the murderer?

Ilya Komanichov had a lot of enemies. Including the Black Russian, who was just as intent on retrieving it as Dimitri.

But none of that mattered as much as one other rather important point. Aidan still had the treasure in his possession. Curse or not, if it was found on him, it would undoubtedly be very bad for his health.

He examined the room, searching for somewhere it could be hidden where Dimitri and his men would not find it. The man was clearly no fool, and would know full well his enemy, or his loyal accomplice, would have hidden it well.

Searching the whole ship would take them some time. From what he'd seen a short while ago, at least six of the eight sailing crew had mutinied. A few of them would be needed to keep the ship sailing, and thoroughly searching every cabin and the guests in them with just a few available men would be a painstaking task that would likely take many hours.

It was little comfort. There was no telling when they would get round to their cabin, and as he turned away and shook his head in frustration, realising there was nowhere to hide the pendant where they wouldn't find it, one other harsh fact of life rammed itself home.

Even if he did hide it, when it was found in the cabin it would be obvious *who* had hidden it.

And powerful Russian mafia families didn't think twice about retribution against those who messed with them.

Dimitri had already proved that.

The door creaked open, and Daisy slipped back into the room. She came straight up to Aidan, and fell into him. Her face was lined with motherly concern.

'I'm worried about Celia, dear. Something like this could set her back weeks,' she whispered into his shoulder.

'I know. But I think we should be worried about all of us, Flower. The situation we're in could set us back a lot more than weeks.'

'I take it you've been looking for a hiding place?' she said, already knowing he'd never find anywhere.

'Looked over every inch of the place. Guess I don't need to tell you there's nowhere they won't search.'

She walked away a few steps. 'Can't you swallow it?'

'Seriously? You've seen the size of the thing. I really don't fancy dying of an internal haemorrhage... and it really would be the Crimson Heart then.'

'Fair point. Bad idea.'

'I guess I could go to Dimitri, give him the thing in exchange for our lives?'

'Oh right. You really think that would work?'

'Not for a moment.'

'Anyway, then you'd incur the voodoo wrath of Tia Dalma, so death might end up being the better option.'

'Are you trying to cheer me up?'

'Well, we've got to do something. Including discovering who actually hung Barbossa.'

He opened his mouth to protest about his wife musing over something that wasn't exactly high on his priority list right then, but suddenly realised having his mind taken off his own perilous situation might not be a bad thing.

'Dimitri looked a little surprised when he saw Ilya hanging there, even though he tried not to show it.'

'Yes, I noticed that too. God only knows how many of Ilya's secret enemies are on the guest list... and then there's Tia.'

'She couldn't have hauled Barbossa up there on her own, surely?'

'Probably not. But these Russian women are strong.'

'She's half-Russian, dear.'

'Even so, I doubt she'd have the kind of strength to overpower him and then pull him up forty feet.'

'Which leaves Davy Jones and his salty men as the likely suspects.'

'Maybe. But they're probably not the only ones.'

'And we're not even allowed on deck, so finding out who killed him isn't going to be easy.'

Daisy sat down heavily on the bed, looked at Aidan with desolate eyes. 'She kissed him, you know.'

'Who... Tia Dalma?'

'*Noo*, you dipstick. Celia. She just told me she went for a walk on deck last night, and Will was there. She ended up kissing him.'

'Oh dear.'

'She went to bed feeling like a million pieces of eight, and then this morning discovered he was one of the mutineers.'

'That's the last thing she needs. More men betraying her feelings.'

'Tell me about it. She's in bits right now. Thank goodness there's no little packets of stuff kicking around here, otherwise I fear the worst.'

He nodded. 'She's at a delicate phase right now for sure. Maybe a good idea we're on a pirate ship... from that point of view anyway. We should maybe ask her to come and join us?'

'I wanted her to come back with me. She said she needed to be alone. I think maybe it's best to give her that space for now, dear? The last thing she needs is two old cronies droning on about how unfair life is.'

'Ok, we'll give her a couple of hours. If any of us actually get a couple of hours. But then we'll go see how she is, ok?'

'I'd go in two minutes. But you're right, as usual. She does need space... but someone ransacking her and her room isn't going to help.'

'I still need to find somewhere to hide this cursed pendant.'

'Give it to me.'

'Dear, I'm not putting you even more at risk.'

'Don't worry, Dip. That particular treasure is your idiotic doing, and your responsibility. But I'm the flame-haired pirate with the devious side, remember?'

He headed over to the chest of drawers, felt in his pyjama pocket and handed Daisy the pendant.

'Lift your pretend sword from the scabbard, Calico.'

'Huh?'

'Just do as I ask, bilge-rat!'

He found a grin. 'I know Anne Bonny and Calico Jack ripped pieces out of each other verbally, but do you have to get that far into character?'

'Just shut your mouth, scum,' she grinned back, dropping the pendant into the scabbard. 'Now put your sword back in, and shove it in place as hard as you can.'

He smiled at the hiding place that was as good as anywhere. 'Yes my dear Anne, I can see now why you eventually disappeared from the face of the Earth, and no one ever discovered where you went.'

Chapter 19

Officer Sarah Lowry slapped her phone back on her desk in the squad room, a frown on her face. It was twelve noon, and Daisy wasn't playing ball.

Ever since they'd left Great Yarmouth, she'd been receiving a constant stream of pictures as requested, making her envious, and wish she was experiencing the action for herself, instead of being stuck at work.

But ever since the previous evening, the pictures had stopped coming. That in itself wasn't the reason for the frown. She'd just decided to call her, ask why the pictures weren't appearing on her phone, and had discovered the reason why.

According to the message that had flashed up on her screen, Daisy's phone was apparently switched off.

That wasn't too worrying either; Daisy might have run out of battery life. It hadn't sat easily... from previous experience she knew Daisy never allowed her phone to die, her training from her earlier life teaching her to never be without a means of communication.

What was more worrying was that Sarah had called Aidan's phone, and discovered it too was switched off. So she'd then called Celia's, and got the same message.

All three phones were switched off. Apparently.

She knew where they'd spend the night, and that they should now be underway on the second leg of their voyage to London. She also knew they hadn't been unreachable at any time on the first leg. Sailing close to the coast, mobile phone networks had no problem reaching the ship.

By now they should be just off the coast of Essex, where network signals were good and strong. There would have been no problem reaching a phone that wasn't switched off.

So why was her call not getting through to any of them?

'You look like you've just been stood up on a date, Lowry.'

She glanced up, saw DCI Burrows looking down at her, a slightly-amused look on his craggy face. 'I wish I had been... well, you know what I mean, sir. I've just called Daisy's phone, and it says it's switched off.'

'Maybe the old codger has finally got tired of you calling her all the time,' he quipped.

'I've only called her twice, sir,' she said, a little curtly. 'But it's unusual for her, so I called Aidan's and Celia's, and they're both apparently switched off too.'

He frowned. 'That's odd. But there might be an explanation. Maybe the Black Pearl is sailing a little further offshore, gone out of range?'

'It's possible. But they should be off the coast of Essex by now, and mobile signals there are really good. And from what I understand, hotel boats have to stay within a certain distance of the shore unless they're licensed for ocean cruises.'

'Yes, they do. But they still might have strayed a bit too far out. Are they under sail?'

She nodded. 'Apparently they're keeping true to the concept, unless there's no wind at all.'

'Unlikely at this time of year.'

'Sir, 'I'm starting to wonder if something has happened?'

He let out a resigned sigh. 'Those two damned wrinklies. Even on a weekend away they still cause me problems. Ok, it's out of our jurisdiction, but I'll call Southend. They might have something that can spot them, put your mind at rest.'

120

'Thank you, sir.'

Half an hour later Burrows called out from his office doorway. 'They've not reached Southend yet, but the webcam at Martello Tower next to Clacton has picked them up. I've patched the live feed into your laptop.'

Sarah lifted the lid, and opened the link. She could see the Black Pearl, sailing close to the shore. The sails were set, and nothing seemed to be amiss.

Burrows came over, watched the feed with her. 'All seems fine, Lowry.'

'But I don't understand, sir. They can't be more than a mile off the coast. There shouldn't be any problem with mobile signals.'

'Yes, it does seem odd. Have you tried again?'

Sarah dialled all three numbers once more. All of them appeared to be switched off. 'They must have ship-to-shore. Can the coastguard call them?'

He let out a sigh. 'I suppose it would put our minds at rest.' He pulled the phone from his jacket pocket, called the Southend station, asked them to give him the local coastguard number.

Then he called that, and asked the harbourmaster to call the ship. For three minutes he waited impatiently, and then the voice on the end spoke.

'Sorry, DCI Burrows. For some reason we can't get through. Radio must be down.'

He glanced to Sarah. The phone was on speaker, she'd heard every word. 'Sir, I don't like this. Too many coincidences.'

He nodded his agreement. 'Much as I hate to admit it, Lowry, I agree. Something's not right.'

'Sir, can we...'

'Get your coat. There's nothing much going on here. Let's get to Southend, see if we can shed any light on the situation from there.'

Sarah took a last look at the screen. From a distance, all seemed fine. Except for the sea. Even close to the shore, it was beginning to swell. It was getting cloudy too; dark clouds laden with late-Autumn rain.

A rough sea was the last thing Daisy and her family needed to make what might be a bad situation even worse.

Chapter 20

It was two in the afternoon when Daisy and Aidan felt the ship shudder for the first time. For a while they'd felt the cabin moving more than it had done before, the rise and fall of the sea starting to lighten their bodies as the ship made the crest of a wave and dropped back down again.

But it was the first time it had dropped back down to the ocean so hard it had made everything shake.

'How's your stomach, dear?' said a slightly-nervous Daisy.

'Fine. But I'm glad you didn't make me swallow the pendant.'

'I'd better go see how Celia is doing.'

'I'll come with you.'

She put a hand on his arm. 'Better stay here, Dip. We're not supposed to leave our cabins, remember? Two of us might be one too many, in more ways than one.'

He nodded his reluctant agreement, and watched as Daisy walked a slightly-wavy path to the door, and disappeared.

Daisy glanced both ways before committing to the fifteen-foot walk to Celia's door. She could hear the sounds of ransacking going on inside two of the cabins on the opposite side of the ship, both their doors wide open.

A woman's voice was protesting loudly. Then she heard the slap of hand against cheek, and the growl of a man's voice. *'Shut up, wench.'*

She made a slight detour and peeped around the doorframe. A man and a woman were standing by the bed looking distraught, their arms around each other. The middle-aged woman was crying hysterically, her husband doing his best to calm her down.

There were two mutineer pirates turning everything upside down. Daisy clenched her fists, forcing herself to keep from whipping her sword from its scabbard and doing the wrong thing. Two dead mutineers would be satisfying, but would only make the situation worse for everyone else.

She could hear similar sounds of searching coming through the other open door. She headed to Celia's door, deciding her daughter needed her more than unfortunate strangers. It seemed like the treasure-seekers were searching in packs of two, and working their way down the starboard cabins before switching to the port side where their cabins were located.

They had a little while yet before the Crimson Heart would be discovered.

Just before Celia's door she felt her body go light, almost levitating itself off the floor. It was a seriously unpleasant feeling, not being able to see the sea in the dimly-lit corridor, or anticipate when they were going to go up and crash back down.

Five seconds later, the ship shuddered and creaked, and her body went heavy. She sucked in a breath to steady already-shattered nerves, and opened Celia's door. She was in bed, but not asleep.

'Hey you, how are you doing?'

'I'm ok,' she said in a small voice. 'I just thought being in bed was the best place, with all the upping and downing.'

'You might be right there,' Daisy smiled, noticing her daughter's slightly red eyes. She sat on the end of the bed. 'But if you want to come and join us, we'd love to have you. It might be a while before they search your cabin; they're working their way down the starboard rooms first.'

Celia sat up. She was still wearing the dress. 'Thanks mum. Maybe later. I'm ok here for now.'

'Your call. But don't stay being upset on your own if you feel you want company.'

'I... I was just wondering what it is with me and men. First it was my so-called boyfriend at uni, who introduced me to drugs and got me hooked so I'd sleep with him. Then Jason Briggs, who saw my dependence and made sure it got worse. Then the black guy...'

'Adde Wambua.'

'Yes, the one who took me. Then came Emmanuel Oyite, who forced me to be his submissive for three years... and now...'

'Will Turner.'

'What is it with men, mum?'

'They're despicable creatures.'

'You did alright with dad.'

'Maybe I was lucky. They're not really all despicable.'

'Just the ones I meet.'

She wiped away a tear. Daisy leant over and gave her a hug. 'Your luck will change. One day a good man will come along.'

'Right now it doesn't feel like it. And that's if we get off this ship alive.'

'I don't think Dimitri has any intention of killing innocent people, dear. He just wants the treasure.'

'And if he can't find it?'

Daisy swallowed hard. Celia had no idea where the booty was. And it had to stay that way. 'I'll protect you, Celia.'

'Will said that.'

'He did? When?'

'When I met him on the deck. He got all nervous and cryptic, and said it just before he disappeared.'

'I see.'

'You see?'

'Perhaps there's more to our Mr. Turner than meets the eye, Elizabeth.'

'That's true enough. He was all dashing charm until the shit hit the fan, and now he's a thug.'

'Maybe.'

Daisy left her daughter in peace, her mind full of the words she'd spoken. There was a possibility Will was a reluctant pirate, persuaded to mutiny because of personal circumstances they didn't know about.

If he was doing things that didn't sit easily, there might be a chance of turning him when push came to shove. It wasn't exactly a problem-solver, but given their current situation, she'd take even the faintest possibility of one pirate doing a double-mutiny.

Chapter 21

Celia was standing by the cannon in her cabin, looking through the gun-port window at the heavy swell and the rain that had just started lashing down, when two of the mutineer pirates burst into the room. They didn't knock, of course.

One of them was Will Turner.

She gave him a glare her mother would have been proud of. 'Mr. Turner. How nice to see you,' she said sarcastically.

'Please don't be like this,' he muttered.

'And why not?'

He looked like he was struggling to answer, but then his companion didn't give him time anyway, making a beeline for the woman he was actually looking forward to body-searching.

Will grabbed him by the arm. 'Leave it. I'll search Miss Swann. You do the en suite.'

For a second he looked like he was going to draw his sword, but then shrugged and went to do as he was told. *'Might have known you'd get all the fun jobs,'* he growled as he disappeared.

Celia smiled a smile she wasn't feeling. 'Shall I strip naked for you, Mr. Turner?'

'I said please don't be like this.'

She ignored that, turned her back on him. 'Help me with the zip, please.'

He seemed like he didn't know quite what to do. 'That... that won't be necessary, Miss Swann.'

She turned back to him. 'Oh, Mr. Turner... all these acres of fabric? I could be concealing all kinds of treasure, could I not?'

He walked up to her, patted her down in a half-hearted kind of way. She shook her head at his reluctance. 'Well I do declare, Will. I seem to be embarrassing you.'

'Look... I'm not exactly happy about this.'

'Then why are you allowing yourself to be so embarrassed?'

'I... that's none of your business.'

'You touch a lady of my standing all over, without my permission, and it's *none of my business*, Mr. Turner?'

The ship lurched violently, throwing them together as they grasped hold of each other to avoid falling over. For a moment their faces were inches apart, and Celia could feel his pained, desolate eyes boring into her.

'So... is there something you want to tell me, Will?'

He pushed himself away, shook his head like the weight of the sea was on it. 'I didn't realise... didn't think about the... I never thought someone would get murdered...'

Celia realised he was wavering, opened her mouth to turn the screw, but didn't get the chance. The other mutineer came back from the en suite, and they weren't alone anymore. 'Nothing there,' he grumbled.

'Nothing here either,' said Will, even though he'd not really searched the room. 'It's clean.'

The pirate didn't look convinced. 'It doesn't look like you've searched very much. *I'll do it...*'

Will began to head for him to try and force him to leave, but suddenly he didn't have to. Through the open door, Mr. Gibbs shout from the staircase did it for him.

'All hands on deck. Storm ahoy.'

The other pirate looked at Will, a strange kind of fear in his eyes. A land-lubbing criminal thug, in a single second he was all at sea.

Will grabbed the opportunity to remove them both from Celia's personal space. 'Come on. We're going to be needed to shorten the sails.'

Just as they left the room, Will glanced back. It was a feeble attempt to defend himself, but it was all he had right then. 'I told you I'd protect you.'

Celia watched them go, a mess of conflicting emotions making her shake her head in confused frustration. She would have liked more time to pump Will, discover just what was going on in his head. The impending storm had saved a humiliating ransacking of both her and the room, but also taken away the chance to get him to see the error of his ways.

He'd obviously been persuaded to be a part of Dimitri's band of merry men, but it clearly wasn't sitting easily. His eyes had been painful to look into, because they'd given away the torment in his head... and probably in his heart.

Perhaps he'd succumbed to the lure of what he thought would be easy money, been told lies about just what was at stake. In their talk on the quarterdeck he'd implied he was just a poor actor.

Then again, if he was a poor petty criminal instead, he was hardly going to admit it to a girl of Elizabeth Swann's standing.

She slumped down onto the bed as the ship crashed back to the bottom of a wave and she felt her body go heavy. Her heart was heavy too, but with fearful confusion, not sadness. The poor actor, or poor criminal known as Will Turner wasn't making any sense.

Was he a good guy, or a bad guy?

Right then there was no way to know.

129

But the one thing she did know was that she didn't fancy being alone anymore. In more than one way they were heading for the eye of the storm, and she didn't wish to face any of those ways on her own.

Chapter 22

'Are you sure that old thing is working right?' said a slightly-fraught Sarah.

The harbourmaster, sitting at the ship-to-shore radio at Leigh-on-Sea harbour, looked at her like he couldn't believe she'd asked. 'With all due respect, Officer Lowry...'

Burrows butted in. 'Of course it's working, Lowry. They use it all the time.'

'Sorry, sir. So why aren't they answering?'

'That's a good question. But it is a possibility they really do have radio problems.'

'You don't actually believe that, sir.'

The harbourmaster saved Burrows the embarrassment of answering. 'We've just broadcast a storm warning to all the shipping in the area. From what you say they're only a mile or so offshore, so they'll not get the brunt of it.' He glanced at his watch. 'It's just gone three. I'm a bit surprised they've not come into view here yet. According to the cruise plan they were required to log, they're due to dock in London in two hours time.'

'Are you saying they're behind schedule, Mr. Williams?' asked Burrows.

'By a good couple of hours. They passed the Felixstowe Docks tower right on schedule.'

Sarah threw a nervous glance to her boss. 'Sir, this is all too worrying. No phone signals still, not answering the radio, and well behind schedule?'

The harbourmaster seemed to agree. 'There's a coastguard vessel only a few miles out from the Blackwater estuary, heading to London. Would you like me to send them to check?'

'Yes please,' said Sarah, before Burrows had the chance to say it.

Sarah and Burrows wandered out onto the quay, walked together right to the point of the harbour. Even at full speed it would be a good half-an-hour until the coastguard met up with the Black Pearl, and there was little for them to do until they got news from them.

They stood next to the beacon, gazing out to the grey sea, and the dark clouds gathering. Significant waves were beginning to crash against the harbour walls, and spots of rain had started to fall.

'Do you think they've hit trouble?' Sarah asked Burrows in a small voice.

'Not legitimate trouble, Lowry. Let's face it, they were only a mile offshore when we saw them on the webcam, and the storm is only just brewing. Even if they were observing radio-silence for some reason, if they were in serious trouble the first thing they'd do was get on the radio.'

'I suppose so.'

'Come on. It's starting to rain heavier. Let's get back to the harbourmaster's office, and keep dry. There could be word from the coastguard any time now.'

They'd only been back in the office five minutes, sipping mugs of hot chocolate, when the radio crackled into life.

'Andy... did you say they were supposed to be heading for London Docklands? Over.'

'According to the cruise plan, Phil. Why? Over.'

'Because we've just got sight of them, about a mile ahead. It looks like they're on short sail, heading towards the Blackwater estuary. Over.'

132

'Maybe they're running for shelter? Over.'

'Possibly. But it's not that big a swell here. A vessel of that size should be able to weather that with no problems. Over.'

'Go and see if they're in trouble, Phil. Stay in contact. Over.'

'On our way now. Should be with them in five minutes. Out for now.'

The harbourmaster glanced to the two police officers. 'I'm no officer of the law, but I'm not convinced all is well. Something's not right here.'

'I agree. But we should know what's what in a few minutes,' said a rather-concerned Burrows.

That few minutes felt like an hour. But then the radio crackled again, and Phil was back.

'Andy, we're just manoeuvring close now. I'm on the portable, in the bows. We're just about to hail them. All looks fine from a hundred yard distance. Over.'

'Be careful, Phil. Over.'

They heard one of the crew calling through an electric loud-hailer. *'Black Pearl... is everything okay? We can't communicate with you.'*

A voice with a Russian accent called back, through an old-fashioned loud-hailer. *'Sorry... radio is out. We're just heading for sheltered waters. We're fine, thank you for your concern. No problems.'*

Then, another voice cried out, in a more frantic kind of way. It sounded like Jack Sparrow's.

'Don't listen to him. We're all hostages, and this wasn't what I signed up for...'

Then silence. After interminable seconds, Phil's voice spoke into the portable radio. *'Um... one of the pirates had*

133

just slapped a hand across his mouth and dragged Jack Sparrow away, Andy. I know this all sounds like a crazy movie.'

'Phil, I don't think it does. Maybe you should back off for now... over.'

'No can do. If there are people at risk, we need to know.'

Then, nobody was left in any doubt what was happening. The voice with the Russian accent was back, its owner realising he'd been given no choice. *'This vessel is under mutiny now. My men and I have over forty hostages. If you don't leave immediately, and keep a total media blanket on this, we will fire on you without hesitation, and start killing the hostages one by one.'*

The coastguard captain didn't seem very willing to just back off. *'Sir, I think you should allow us to come aboard.'*

The harbourmaster groaned, realising the coastguard crew were in a bad situation. 'Phil, back off...'

He didn't get any further. They heard the Russian voice snarl out, '*I did warn you.'*

Then something happened no one could have predicted. There was a loud bang, and moments later, through the radio they heard something sear into the water just in front of the bow of the boat. And then one second later, Phil's disbelieving voice trembling through the radio.

'Jesus Christ... they're firing on us.'

Burrows snatched the mike from the harbourmaster. 'This is DCI Burrows. Back off now. What kind of weapons have they got?'

'You're not going to believe this, sir.'

'Just tell me what you know, Phil.'

'Um... we've just been fired on by a pirate cannon.'

134

Sarah was scanning the huge map of the local coastline fixed to the wall of the office. Hearing the Russian accent coming through the coastguard's radio had rung a vague bell, and she was starting to wonder if fantasy and harsh reality were coming together in a rather perilous way.

Burrows walked over and stood behind her, as she traced a route over the map with her finger. He could see the steam coming out of her ears. 'What are you thinking, Lowry?'

'I know Ilya Komanichov is Russian, but...'

'But what?'

'But he's hardly likely to seize his own boat, is he?'

'Fair point.'

'So something else is going down. And I think I know what it might be.'

'You going to let us mere mortals in on the secret?'

She grinned to her boss, turned back to the harbourmaster. 'Andy, ask Phil what the guy who shouted the threats looked like, please?'

Burrows shook his head. 'Lowry, they're all in costume... no-one's going to look like who they really are...'

'Well, you never know. Daisy sent me a pic of Ilya dressed as Barbossa, so if it was him then we'll know one fact of life.'

The radio crackled, as Phil replied to the harbourmaster's question. *'Scary looking chap, Andy, but he didn't seem to be wearing any kind of costume on his head. Cropped hair, square jaw, designer stubble, 'bout late forties.'*

Sarah glanced to Burrows. 'That sure as hell isn't Komanichov. He's in his sixties, with longish wavy silver hair.'

135

'How do you know all this? Russian crime families are hardly our jurisdiction.'

'Don't you read the news?'

'Only when we're in it. Other than that, just the football pages.'

She shook her head. 'Well if you did keep abreast of what's going on outside Kings Lynn, you'd know Komanichov made a big show of putting a valuable pendant in Barfly's vault recently. The word is he stole it from another crime family who had stolen it from the Moscow State Museum not so long ago, but no one dared try and prove any of it.'

'I'm confused...'

'All you need to understand is that I'm now wondering if the pendant wasn't actually put in the safe. Barfly's was broken into last week, a lot of stuff stolen from the vault. Bit of a coincidence, don't you think?'

'For sure. But what does any of that have to do with the Black Pearl?'

'Get your brain in gear... sir. Komanichov's daughter is getting married in a few days. He was reported as wanting the pendant to be safe until he could give it to her as a wedding gift. So if he was so jittery about it being safe, why did he make a show of telling everyone exactly where it was?'

'Because it was actually somewhere else... *oh...*'

'Now you see it.'

'I'm starting to see one possibility.'

'Komanichov is keeping it on him until the wedding day. He knows he can't trust anyone. But someone... maybe the family he stole it from... knows what's going on. And what better place to steal it back than a ship out at sea?'

136

'They've still got to get onto dry land with the treasure though.'

'I know. That's why I'm looking at the map. Phil said it looked like they were heading for the Blackwater estuary.'

'Christ, that's a good five miles wide at the entrance.'

'And look... if you follow it inland towards Maldon for a few miles, there's about a million secluded coves and bays where there could be a car waiting for them in the next few hours.'

'And they've got multiple hostages as insurance.'

Sarah nodded, knowing full well the authorities couldn't do a thing that would endanger the lives of those on board. Novalenko had already warned them to keep it out of the media, and that if they tried to interfere, lives would be lost. And she had no doubt the man who made that threat would have no problem carrying it out.

They had no idea where the Black Pearl would make land. On the green and pleasant coastline of both sides of the wide estuary, it could be anywhere. Even if they got a police chopper to follow it from a distance, it would only take a minute or two for the ship to cruise far enough into a bay in the middle of nowhere, so they could escape.

And for sure, they'd take a few hostages with them as getaway insurance.

Burrows ran a nervous hand across his mouth. 'Hell's bells, this is a genius plan. If we alert the powers that be, there's no communication with the ship so they'll have no choice but to storm it, and it'll be a bloodbath for sure. Right now it's just us and the coastguard vessel that knows anything about this. And if we want to avoid serious loss of life, it might have to stay that way for the next few hours.'

Sarah pointed to something on the map. 'It would help if we knew the location where they're making land, sir.'

'So why are you pointing at a sailing club just inside the estuary?'

'If we alert the authorities, god-knows-who will take over. And you know what that will lead to, sir.'

'And?'

'There are good friends of mine in danger on the Black Pearl, and in the immediate future it's up to us. I've got a bit of an idea, sir. But you're not going to like it.'

Chapter 23

Daisy and Aidan could see land in the distance, through their gun-port window on the port side of the boat. They shouldn't be able to see land on that side of the boat, not until they reached the Thames estuary.

'Well dear, either we've travelled at supersonic speed through this storm, or we're taking the scenic route,' she said.

'Hmm... looks like we're heading for the Blackwater estuary.'

'And how would you know that?'

'The power of deduction from a galactic-sized brain, Flower. Judging by the approximate speed of the vessel on short sail, and the distance we must have travelled, and computing the map of the Essex coastline into my photographic memory... and the fact we're sure as hell not going to dock in the Port of London...'

'Wish I hadn't asked now.'

'Quite honestly dear, I don't know if it is the Blackwater, but it would be logical.'

'Why?'

'Because for miles until it reaches Maldon there are wild and hilly bits, and there's a lot of difficult to get to secluded coves our pirates could anchor in and escape.'

'But they haven't got the booty yet,' said Celia, sitting on the end of the bed.

Aidan nodded. 'No, and this rough weather has stopped them searching, all of them needed on deck. It's a skeleton crew for this type of vessel at the best of times.' He glanced at the ancient-looking but very modern clock on the wall. 'It's five now. Be getting dark in a couple of hours. And after that... um, altercation with the coastguard, it doesn't seem like anyone's going to risk coming to help.'

Daisy looked thoughtful. From their window, they'd had a good view of the coastguard vessel coming close, and then heard the bang above their heads as Dimitri had fired a cannon at them to make a point.

They'd seen the cannonball smack into the water just in front of the boat, and Daisy had shrieked at Aidan...

'I thought these cannons were fake?'

Aidan had said in an equally-shocked way... 'The ones in the guest cabins are fake. But there's two either side of the quarterdeck. I thought they looked older than the others. They're clearly not fake.'

'I think the coastguard would agree with you, dear,' she'd answered.

Then they'd watched as the coastguard had withdrawn to a mile distance, but now even their vessel had disappeared, at least from their sight.

Daisy had *that* look in her eye. 'We've got to find out where they're heading, dear.'

'Why? We can't call hostage-line and let them know where we're making land, can we?'

'No, but if there's some way to scupper the ship?'

'Seriously? You want to sink the ruddy thing with us on board?'

'Noo... just hamper their progress, help whoever it is who's coming to rescue us.'

'Mum... you really think SWAT is going to parachute in, with forty hostages at the mercy of the Russian mafia?'

Daisy ran shaking fingers through her flame-haired wig. 'Ok, maybe no one is coming to rescue us. They know it'll be a bloodbath. Out on the water like we are, no one can burst through the door and take them by surprise, can they?'

'So that line of Daisy thinking is futile then,' said Aidan.

'Maybe. But we've got to do something. 'I'm going up on deck, see what I can find out.'

'Dear, they said to stay in the cabins...'

'I know. And I'm going stir-crazy. You two stay here.'

'Mum...'

Celia's pleading was too late. Daisy was already out of the door, bouncing off the corridor walls as the motion of the boat caught her off-guard for a moment.

She swallowed hard, closed her eyes to try and recover her balance. It wasn't easy, in a narrow corridor with no windows that felt like a fairground ride. She shook away the crazy thought that a skeleton waving a skull-and-crossbones would appear from nowhere, and tried to convince herself she wasn't really going crazy.

As if being a hostage on the Black Pearl pirate ship, seized by Davy Jones and his salty crew, wasn't crazy enough.

No one was around below deck. She stumbled her way towards the staircase, climbed the steps gingerly and poked her head just above the deck line. Straightaway she saw three of the crew pulling on halyards, fighting to keep the half-furled sails at their correct angle to the fierce wind. The rain was lashing down, the bare bits of their skin glistening as they worked away.

Up on the quarterdeck, a fourth crewmember was struggling with the wheel, doing his best to keep the ship on course through the storm. For a minute she watched, spotting no one else except one more crew member towards the stern of the boat, working away on something

141

at the aft mast. He was too far away for her to see who it was.

She flicked her head from left to right. She could see land on both sides, a couple of miles away. It looked like Aidan was right; they were heading into the Blackwater estuary. And because of the foul weather, it was getting dark earlier than it should.

She was just about to head back to the dry and warm cabin when two other people came into view, just a few feet away from the staircase hatch. She slunk back against the support post, trying to hear if they said anything.

It wasn't difficult. They had to shout to hear each other through the rain and the wind, and every word drifted through to the staircase.

Mr. Gibbs was the first to speak. *'With all due respect, captain, there's only five cabins left to search. The men have ransacked everywhere else on this ship, and there's still no sign of it.'*

'So what are you saying, Mr. Gibbs?' Dimitri didn't sound too happy with life.

'I'm sayin' sir, if we don't find it by the time we reach Blackwater Bay, perhaps it's time to accept the Crimson Heart isn't here?'

'It is here,' Dimitri snapped.

'With all due respect, captain... what if it isn't?'

'Then you and your men receive nothing, Mr. Gibbs. Is that what you want?'

'Um... no, sir. But we was promised payment regardless of the outcome...'

'You know the rules, Mr. Gibbs. No treasure, no payday.'

'But, with all...'

'Enough. Let us get through this storm, and then I suggest you find the pendant... or you'll discover there are worse things than peasant curses to deal with.'

Daisy staggered back to the cabin, a slight smile on her face. By a quirk of fate the captain and his number two had stood in exactly the right place for her to eavesdrop, and the foul weather that had saved them from being searched earlier, had also meant they'd had to shout to be heard.

And anyone eavesdropping on the conversation now knew where the ship was heading, and that neither the rank and file nor the self-imposed captain were exactly happy with life.

Chapter 24

'This is insanity, Lowry,' said Burrows as he wrapped a nervous hand around his mouth.

'I agree,' said the commander of the sailing club. 'I wouldn't allow any of my members to go out in this weather.'

'I'm not one of your members,' said Sarah huffily, as she strapped a lifejacket around her body.

'That's not the point, and you know it, officer.'

'Look commander, the British police are commandeering this sailing dinghy, so what we do with it is not your concern.'

'Putting lives at risk *is* my concern,' he said huffily, realising he was sailing against the wind.

'Lowry, I could order you to be sensible, for once,' said Burrows, a little desperately.

'Sir... my dear friends' lives are at risk. Are you really going to *order* me to ignore that?'

'No, but there must be another way. What exactly do you think you'll achieve?'

'There is no other way, sir. And... and I don't quite know yet what I'm going to achieve until I get there, except to be with them, and let them know they're not alone.'

'If you don't drown first,' said the commander, making a good point.

'*Will you shut up about drowning?*'

'Actually, it's the first time I've mentioned it...'

'*Oooh...*' Sarah shook her head in an annoyed kind of way, and began to push the dinghy on its dolly towards the slipway. 'I could do with a hand to launch this thing, sir?'

Burrows shook his head, realising his rookie officer wasn't going to take no for an answer, and would actually launch it by herself if he refused to help. He wrapped his hands around the starboard gunwhale, and pushed the little boat to the slipway.

Just before she climbed into the dinghy, Sarah wrapped a hand around his arm. 'Thank you, sir. It'll be fine. My dad and me have sailed these things on The Wash ever since I was a little girl. I know how to handle a sailing dinghy.'

'It's not your ability, or the heavy sea, that worries me, Lowry.'

'I know, sir. But... but I just have to be there. Can you understand that?'

He nodded reluctantly. 'Amazingly I can, yes. Please be super careful.'

Sarah smiled. Then she turned away, so her boss couldn't see her swallow nervously. She'd been honest enough about her sailing trips out on The Wash next to Kings Lynn, but she hadn't admitted that her father had never allowed them to sail if the sea was anything but well calm.

Out on a rough sea, on her own, was going to be a whole new experience.

And one that relied totally on the mutineers having enough compassion to rescue a lone sailor who'd got herself into trouble.

– – –

Daisy, Aidan and Celia had just finished a meal that had been brought to their cabin by the frightened serving wench who had waited on them in the Tortuga bar. The kitchen staff was taking meals to the guests, so they didn't have to starve.

Not a part of the mutineer pirate crew, they were just as terrified as those they were serving. Daisy had pumped the girl to see if she knew anything they didn't, but other than telling them the cabin search was not going to resume until first light the next morning, she was just as much in the dark.

The sun was just dropping behind the low hills of the land a mile or so away. The movement of the ship had lessened, the swell beginning to dissipate. Eating a meal without the food lifting off the plate was something of a relief.

Then they heard the sound of running footsteps on the deck above their heads, and the muffled sound of men shouting. Daisy immediately thought the obvious. 'Oh my god... the police are not mounting some kind of rescue attempt, are they? The idiots...'

They listened nervously for a minute or two. Still they could hear muffled shouts, but there was no sound of gunfire or fighting.

'Guys, what's going on?' said Celia.

'I don't know, but something's happening. I'm going to see what it is.'

'Dear...' Aidan protested, but Daisy was already at the door, so he and Celia shook resigned heads and followed her.

As they reached the deck, several of the crew were shouting at something in the water off the starboard side of the ship. They couldn't see what it was, the hull blocking their view, so they ran to the deck rail. No one stopped them, the crew all too busy with whatever it was they were shouting instructions to.

It *was* a rescue attempt, but the other way round. The crew were rescuing the police, not that they knew it.

Will Turner was climbing over the rail, onto a ladder built into the hull, a grappling hook on a long pole in one hand. Drifting towards them, just ten metres away, was a tiny sailing dinghy with a single occupant aboard. She was female, a scarf knotted under her chin, topped with a peaked cap with what looked like the emblem of a sailing club on it.

The boat looked a little the worst for wear, its single sail ripped from the aluminium boom, flapping away uselessly in the strong wind.

Celia smiled to her mother. 'At least they have enough compassion to save a distressed soul.'

Daisy nodded, watched as the dinghy came to within a few feet of the boat, and Will grabbed it with the grappling hook. The frightened girl scrambled to the bows, and he took her hand and helped her towards the ladder.

She glanced up to the faces watching the rescue. And even thought she was well covered by the scarf, and the light was fading rapidly, Daisy let out a little gasp. Luckily none of the crew noticed her reaction.

'Dears, don't let on you recognise her, but I think we know who that particular lost soul is,' she whispered.

Dimitri didn't look too pleased he'd acquired one extra hostage. He'd been in his quarters when the rescue took place, otherwise it might never have happened at all. He looked the stranded sailor up and down.

'You will stay aboard this ship tonight. We will not be making land until tomorrow morning.'

'Fine by me,' Sarah grinned, playing the slightly-dotty posh sailor. 'Must confess I'd never expected to be rescued by the Black Pearl!'

'Frisk her, Mr. Gibbs.'

147

'Sorry?'

Dimitri shook his head at the puzzled-looking girl. 'The safety of our guests is paramount... miss..?'

'duMaurier. *Soo* pleased to meet you.' She held out a hand, shook his a little too vigorously.

Dimitri looked a tad taken-aback by the gushing. 'Yes, well... we will find somewhere...'

Celia bustled her way to them, put an arm around Sarah. 'Miss duMaurier can stay in my cabin tonight. There's only me in it. Now if you don't mind, this poor woman needs to get dried out.'

She led Sarah away before Dimitri could object, and together they headed down the stairs, followed by Daisy and Aidan. As soon as they were out of hearing range, Daisy let rip.

'*What the hell, Sarah?* Are you totally insane? And... du Maurier? Daphne is it? Or maybe it should be Rebecca, seeing as we're around water. That didn't end happily either.'

Sarah spun round, her eyes flaring anger. 'Sometimes I wonder why I bother worrying so much about you, Daisy Morrow. I risk drowning to come and be with you, and all I get is literary abuse?'

'I...'

Celia looked almost as angry. '*Mum*... try showing a little gratitude for once, ok?'

They were at her door. And three seconds later the two girls were inside, slamming it in Daisy's face.

'I think that told you, dear,' said Aidan.

Daisy covered her face with her hands, and then glanced up desolately to the wooden ceiling. 'I just... all she's done is walk into a perilous situation, Dip. She can't do anything the rest of us can't. She's put her life in danger, for nothing.'

He pulled her close, held her tight, saw the tears of frustration in her eyes. 'Maybe not nothing, dear. Sarah's interventions have made a difference a few times in the recent past... including saving our lives, and rescuing the situation on more than one occasion. Maybe she's got something up her literary sleeve? I suggest we get ourselves back to our cabin, and leave the girls to their own version of girl-power for a while.'

Celia turned on the shower, as Sarah ripped off her soaking wet clothes, and padded into the en suite in just her headscarf.

'Mum didn't mean it, you know. She just tells it like it is, and hang the consequences.'

'It's not exactly what you want to hear though, right after you've intentionally drifted helplessly for two hours in a rough sea.'

'Yeah, I can see that. But mum kind of had a point. Why did you put yourself through that just to get on board?'

Sarah lowered her head. 'Maybe I got jealous of you guys living it up on the Black Pearl.'

'Oh, really?'

'No, of course not. I wanted to be with you, going through hell like you are.'

'How did you even know we were going through hell?'

Sarah grinned. 'Your mum told me.'

'What? How?'

'Well, indirectly I suppose. She'd been sending me loads of pics, but then suddenly they stopped. I tried to call all three of your phones, and they were all dead.'

'They've got some kind of signal jammer.'

'We realised that. So have they found it yet?'

'What?'

'The Crimson Heart.'

'Is that the treasure they're looking for? You seem to know more than I do... and you worked it all out?'

'I am a police officer with a big brain.'

'Don't you start.'

'Fabulous dress by the way, Elizabeth.'

'Thank you. Tell me more facts, please.'

'Ok, I put two and two together, given who the Black Pearl belongs to, and then we were listening in to that Russian voice shouting to the coastguard, so then two and two made a definite four, and then I decided I had to come, and...'

'Ok... I get the point. So who knows about this?'

'Just me and Burrows, and the coastguard vessel that's sitting about a mile away. Kovalenko said to keep a media blanket on it, or he'd kill the hostages, so right now it's just us. So have they found it?'

'Doesn't seem like it. We were told they were going to search the remaining cabins at first light. But I can tell you one thing you don't know. Barbossa's dead.'

'Oh hell. How?'

'Someone hung him from the yardarm.'

'*Seriously?* You don't know who?'

'Most likely Dimitri. But he looked a little surprised when he saw him hanging there.'

Sarah shook her head. 'You're starting to talk like a pirate, Elizabeth. Like being hung from the yardarm is an occupational hazard.'

'I guess this role-play gets under your skin. You going to take that scarf off and get in the shower before the onset of pneumonia?'

'Sure. Not that it could get any wetter.' Sarah glanced furtively around. 'Are there any spy cameras in the cabins?'

'I don't think so. There can't be any in the en suite. You afraid of voyeurs, Sarah? You're already naked apart from that scarf.'

'Not voyeurs. Just Russian spies.'

She lifted the scarf away from her head. Sarah gasped. What looked like a hearing aid sat in her left ear, and as she watched in amazement, Sarah swung out a tiny microphone that was hinged back behind her head, the whole thing hidden by her hair and the scarf.

She grinned cheekily, and spoke quietly into it. 'Sir... come in, sir... is this working?'

Then through the earpiece, came the voice that made the grin even wider.

'Bloody hell, Lowry. Thank god you're safe. And yes, incredibly, it is working.'

'Brilliant, sir. I'm on board, in Celia's cabin. The bad guys don't suspect a thing... I don't think. Just about to get in the shower and warm up. I'll contact you again in a short while. Over and out.'

Celia shook her head, like she couldn't quite believe what was happening. 'You crafty bitch. But how is that working when nothing else is?'

'It uses an SSB band. We had no idea if their blocker jammed all frequencies, or just the ones mobile devices use.'

'I guess now we know.'

'Thank goodness. Isn't this exciting?'

'Maybe not the word I'd use. Get yourself in that shower. I'll go fetch mum and dad, and then we can decide what to do next.'

Chapter 25

A slightly-stunned Daisy and Aidan were waiting for Sarah as she emerged from the en-suite, wrapped in a giant white towel.

'You're still insane... but I'm glad you are.' Daisy gave her a hug. 'I'm sorry I said what I did, Sarah. But I'm feeling a bit helpless right now, and as you know that doesn't sit easily with me.'

'It's ok, I understand. But now we can communicate with Burrows, so if we can find out where they're going to make land, we can apprehend them.'

'Blackwater Bay.'

Sarah grinned. 'I guess I should have realised you'd already know.'

'I snuck up close to the deck, overheard Davy Jones and Mr. Gibbs talking. They mentioned where they were going to make land.'

'Davy Jones?'

'Sorry, Dimitri. He had a Davy Jones mask when he first appeared.'

'Creepy thing,' Celia shuddered.

'Jack Sparrow threw it overboard. So now he looks like the head of a Russian mafia family in a pirate coat.'

'Jack Sparrow not one of the mutineers then?'

'No,' said Aidan. 'But rather like his counterpart, he's not a lot of use.'

'He can handle a sword though,' said Celia sadly.

Sarah glanced to her. 'That sounds like a story is lurking there somewhere.'

'You could put it that way.'

Daisy stopped that conversation in its tracks. 'Sarah, is there anything else to your plan?'

'Not really. Until we got the actual facts, there wasn't much we could plan.'

Daisy wafted away the steam coming out of her ears. 'Ok, well you already deduced correctly what this is all about. In a nutshell, they haven't found the treasure yet, and I rather suspect they won't make land until they do. The storm has gone, and we're cruising slowly up the Blackwater estuary on half-sail, but before too long they're going to have to drop anchor and stop for the night.'

'It won't be Blackwater Bay though. That's where they're getting off and being met, so they're hardly going to advertise that fact several hours before they clear off,' Aidan mused.

'No, definitely not. They'll anchor offshore somewhere, knowing they're safe as houses with all the hostages, then search the remainder of the cabins when it's light enough.'

'I guess it's a possibility the Crimson Heart isn't on board though.'

'Oh, it's onboard for sure, dear.'

'You can't be certain of that.'

Aidan admitted everything. 'Yes, she can. I've got it.'

Sarah and Celia gaped open-mouthed at the revelation that turned them into statues. Finally Celia found her voice.

'You... you had it all this time?'

He lowered his head, spoke quietly and humbly. 'Ilya only invited us so he could entrust me with the Crimson Heart... the last person anyone would suspect was carrying it. Ilya being Ilya, he threatened us with our lives if I didn't do as he asked. So I did as he asked.'

'Oh dad... you should have told me.'

'He didn't even tell *me*,' said Daisy grouchily. 'Not until I accidentally discovered it, and he had no choice.'

'I wanted to protect you all. I got myself into it, and I didn't want anyone else involved.'

Celia gave him a hug. 'You still should have told us.'

'Well, I considered it... but you know what your mother is like...'

'And what's that supposed to mean?' growled Daisy.

'Mum... you know exactly what you're like. You'd have gutted Dimitri, and then we'd all have suffered.'

'I suppose you have a point. I do wish I'd smuggled my automatic rifle onboard though.'

'See what I mean?' said Aidan.

It was Sarah's turn to kill a particular conversation. 'Ok, character assassination is not getting us anywhere. I need to communicate with Burrows, tell him where we're making land tomorrow, so he can get organised. But you say at first light they're searching the remaining cabins, so how do we stop them finding the treasure? Where have you hidden it?'

'Maybe best you two don't know,' said Daisy.

'Mum...'

'I'm serious. Then, even if they threaten you with walking the plank, you can't tell them.'

'Daisy!'

'I'm exaggerating. That'll never happen.'

'Like being hung from the yardarm didn't happen, I suppose?' said Celia indignantly.

'Hmm... that's something else. We still haven't found out who did that.'

'Mum?'

'We've got to make life hard for them. Give them too much to think about.'

'And how do we do that?'

'Find the signal jammer, for starters. If we can destroy that, then everyone will be able to communicate what's going on, and that'll cause all kinds of mayhem.'

Just as Daisy said that, they heard the rasping clunks of the anchor chain. Celia ran to the gun-port window. 'We've stopped. Looks like we're anchoring a half-mile offshore somewhere.'

'As we suspected,' said Aidan. 'I doubt we're far from Blackwater Bay, but we're going to spend the night here, and then get ransacked at first light.'

'Which means we don't have long to make life hard for them. I say we all get some sleep, and then a couple of hours before dawn we head for the bottom of the ship, find that jammer and stick a sword into it or something. Then decide what else we can do to disrupt their lives.'

'We need to be careful though, dear. Dimitri is already frustrated because he's spending an unexpected extra night aboard, having not found the treasure yet. If we piss him off too much, he might freak out and start killing people.'

'That's a good point. But I fear if he doesn't find the pendant, it still won't bode well for anyone, regardless. And if he does find it, it sure won't bode well for you.'

'Thanks for telling it like it is, Flower.'

'Just saying what you already know, darling. So on that note, let's set our alarms for four in the morning, and get some sleep. We can't go a-disrupting if we're exhausted!'

Chapter 26

Daisy wasn't finding anything that could be called proper sleep. Their perilous situation, and the fact that making life hard for Dimitri and his mutineers had a fifty-fifty chance of backfiring, meant what passed for sleep wasn't exactly satisfying.

Aidan was spark out next to her, the fear of the Crimson Heart being discovered in their cabin having the opposite effect to Daisy's lack of sleep. It had brought him a strange kind of exhaustion, which somehow managed to transfer itself to real sleep.

She smiled as she gazed at him, glad he at least had been able to find sleep... although in truth it was sleep that had found him. If he could have stayed awake, he surely would have, desperate to do the impossible and protect his family.

His decisions had been the cause of their life-threatening situation, but she still couldn't blame him for being the nicest of human beings and giving people the benefit of the doubt, even when perhaps the doubt outweighed the benefit.

Daisy closed her eyes, tried again for sleep. It was one in the morning, and in less than three hours, a short while before it started to get light, they were going to risk it all and sneak down to the guts of the ship, and do a few things that definitely had unpredictable consequences.

But as she'd told the others, she couldn't just sit back and do nothing. And she did possess a very real, and very sharp sword.

She wasn't sure if she'd drifted off, or even if the tiny sounds reaching her ears were part of a dream or not. But as she forced consciousness to pull itself together, the sounds were still there.

The room was dark, the only light coming from a bright moon shining over the water, a shaft of yellow light filtering through the gun-port window. Daisy opened her eyes, but didn't move. Lying on her side facing the fast-asleep Aidan, her back was towards the door, where the sounds were coming from.

Tiny sounds, familiar to her. The sounds of a lock being picked.

The sword sat next to her, leaning against the wall in the tiny space between the four-poster and the bedside table, ready for instant action. Yet somehow it didn't feel like it would be needed.

Mutineer pirates who had the entire ship at their mercy didn't bother picking locks.

Whoever was about to come in sure wasn't one of the bad guys. But who was it? Celia and Sarah would just tap the door is there was a problem, surely?

Daisy could feel her heart thumping, as whoever it was finished picking, and the door creaked open. She heard the almost-silent footsteps padding towards the bed as she pretended she was asleep, bracing herself to spin round and grab the sword if it became necessary.

For ten agonising seconds nothing happened. Then, the end of the mattress sank lower, as a butt sat down on it. Still Daisy didn't move, but then a voice spoke quietly.

'Do not pretend to be asleep, Daisy Morrow.'

Daisy turned on her back, looked at the woman sitting on the end of the bed. 'No fooling you is there, Irina Novichocopopolov?'

She smiled in the darkness. 'No. I am top Russian agent for last three years. And you are one of the few people who have no trouble pronouncing my name.'

Daisy pulled herself up gently, not wishing to wake Aidan until she had to. 'RSS? I thought you worked solo?'

'How long you stopped watching me?'

'I retired from MI6 completely eleven years ago.'

'Yes, I thought you looked too old. Since you stopped watching me, Vladimir admitted defeat, made me unofficial member of RSS, as long as I kept my dissidence away from Russian government and focussed on crime families instead. So apart from odd job for him, I am still my own bosses.'

'So you're still feared by the Russian mafia... and still known as the Black Russian?'

She smiled again. 'I like my nick. For that I thank some smart-arse agent in the CIA.'

'It suits you, for sure. Kind of wish I'd come up with it myself.'

'*Ush*... you soft Brits would likely have given me codename like Dark Angel or some such.'

'Kind of like that too... being Brit. But names aside, um... *what the hell are you doing in my bedroom?*'

'Saving your husband's sorry ass.'

'I can save his sorry ass, thank you.'

'You sure about that?'

'Well, not exactly. But I have a sharp sword, see?' Daisy nodded to the weapon leaning against the wall.

'You wish for needle in haystack, stupid old woman?'

'Hey, less of the old, please. And the stupid, come to that. I'm actually neither.'

'How many years you have?'

'Seventy-one. Look, can you get to the point, please?'

'Then you are old woman.'

'The reason you broke in, please?'

'I tell you. To save Aidan's sorry ass.'

'And I told you...' Daisy stopped the words coming out, glanced to the ceiling in frustration. 'Ok, so what makes you think you can save my husband's sorry ass when I can't?'

'In few hours time they will search this cabin. When they find it, he will be severely punished.'

'So what might *it* be?'

Irina threw an impatient arm into the air. 'Don't play stupid old cronie with me, Daisy.'

'You're insulting me again.'

'No... you insult me. You know exactly what I talk about. And if you don't give it me now, it will be curtain for your husband.'

'Curtains.'

'Now you insult my English?'

'Ok, ok. So what happens when they search you?'

Irina shook her head, like it was a ridiculous question. 'They will not search me.'

'Really.'

'I am a ghost, remember?'

'You...' again Daisy halted the retort, looked at the Black Russian for a full ten seconds like she was trying to decide if she was still dreaming or not, and then prodded Aidan. *'Hey, Dip...* wake up. We've got a visitor.'

He groaned, but didn't seem like he wanted to be disturbed, so she poked him a little harder. 'Dear, get yourself awake. We have a visitation.'

Finally he turned over, forced open bleary eyes. 'What... oh, hi Irina.'

'Hi Irina? There's a ghost Black Russian in our bedroom, and that's all you can say?'

'I'm dreaming, right?'

159

'No dear, that vision of loveliness is real... I think.'

He pushed himself up with his elbows, leant back against the plush headboard and rubbed his eyes. 'So she is.'

'She's come to relieve you of the treasure.'

'Um... what treasure?'

'Time to give it a rest, dear. She knows... somehow.'

Irina looked like she was getting even more impatient. 'So, we met again, mister accountant. Now you give me Crimson Heart, ok? So I save your sorry ass.'

'I don't have a sorry ass.'

'You give it me or not?'

'Um... maybe. What if they find it on you?'

Daisy realised things were repeating themselves, and it wasn't pleasing Irina. 'Dear, maybe we should just give it to her? Then at least your sorry ass will be saved.

'Don't you start.'

Aidan flicked the switch on the fake candle-holder, and a low light palled across the bed. He scrambled out from under the duvet, pulled his fake sword from its scabbard, and tipped it upside down, shook it a little to dislodge the pendant. It tumbled out onto the end of the bed.

He picked it up, handed it to Irina. 'I still think it's dangerous for you to have it.'

'*Ush*... it is not your concern. They will not find it on me.'

'So what do you intend doing with it, if we all get off this death ship alive?'

'That is not your concern either. But I will tell you, because I like you. It will go back where it belongs.'

'The Moscow State Museum?'

She slipped the pendant around her neck, made sure it was hidden by the dress of autumn colours and the beads she was already wearing. 'Now I must go, leave you to sleeps.'

160

She walked towards the door. Daisy, still determined to solve the mystery of who committed murder, called after her., 'Irina, as you seem to know everything, who hung Barbossa from the yardarm?'

She paused in the doorway, and suddenly Tia Dalma was back.

'Him cursed.'

'Oh come on, don't give me the old Jamaican sorceress routine. I'm really not that stupid.'

'You tink it is all nonsense, old woman?'

'Now you're insulting me again.'

'You dismiss curse like it nothin' important, then ye *is* stupid old woman.'

Daisy sighed. 'Well, I suppose you of all people should know about such things, Tia.'

She narrowed her black eyes. 'Believe it. Now it may be dat curse is lifted from your husband. Time will tell.'

'May be?' said a wide-eyed Aidan.

Tia Dalma didn't answer. Like so many times before, she was gone, like she was never there at all.

Chapter 27

The alarm on Daisy's phone let out a merry jingle. A weary arm reached out to the bedside table, and a flailing finger flicked the switch to turn it off.

Daisy and Aidan sat up together, before the need to sleep took them away again. The clock on the wall, illuminated by a shaft of moonlight, said three-forty-five.

'You ready for this, dear?' whispered Daisy.

He found a grin. 'This night can't get any more weird, Flower... not after being visited by the ghost of Tia Dalma.'

'You still feel cursed?'

He climbed out of bed. 'You still trying to be funny?'

'I'm not sure any more, Calico,' said Daisy as she slipped on her Anne Bonny clothes, and hitched the sword back into its scabbard.

'With you on that one. What seemed amusing once feels like it's deadly serious now.'

'Please leave the word *deadly* out of that.'

Daisy glanced out of the gun-port window to make sure the dawn was still two hours away. '*Seriously?* You have got to be kidding me...' she exclaimed.

The moon had moved low in the sky, looking larger than ever. Casting a shaft of light across the gently-rippling water, it was doing a very good job of illuminating something else.

One of the big lifeboats was on the move, a single, tricorned figure silhouetted in it, rowing away frantically for his life.

'That lily-livered, cowardly waste of space...' Aidan breathed angrily.

'Saving his own skin, just like his real self,' said Daisy.

'Real?'

'You know what I mean. Our Jack Sparrow seems to be re-enacting another bit of the movie, rowing for his freedom.'

'Maybe we should get on one of those top-deck cannons, sink the cowardly sod.'

'Dear, nothing would give me greater pleasure, but I think cannon fire would very likely wake everyone up, which would defeat our objective, don't you reckon?'

'Damn it. You're right. I suppose we'll have to let him get away with getting away.'

'Sadly, yes. Let's go do what we woke up early to do.'

They tapped gently on the door to Celia's cabin. In seconds she and Sarah were in the corridor with them. Daisy crept to the staircase, climbed a few steps and poked her head just above the deck line. She couldn't see anyone, the mutineer crew likely asleep until first light, knowing their hostages were trying to do the same in their cabins, too terrified to try anything as brave as escaping.

The sails were furled, and all seemed to be at peace. If they didn't know any different, it looked just like the Black Pearl was spending an extra night, anchored a little way offshore, having sheltered from the storm that had now passed.

She hurried back to the others, whispered that no one was around. They already knew the crew's sleeping quarters were in the bows of the ship, accessed by a separate ladder that dropped down from the forecastle. There was unlikely to be any access from there to the bottom of the ship.

The four of them made their way to the rear of the corridor, where another, steeper staircase led to the guts of the ship. Hanging over the first step was a weathered wood sign that said *Authorised Pirates Only*.

They ignored that, climbed down to a small foyer with three doors leading off. One was marked *Galley*, another labelled as the stores. Sarah poked her head around the stores door, flicked on a very modern-looking light, and cast her eyes around.

'*Nothing there, guys,*' she whispered. '*Just store-type stuff.*'

'*That's the engine room,*' said Aidan, pointing to the third door.

'*And how would you know that, dear?*' Daisy grinned.

'*Because it says Engine Room on it.*'

'*Your powers of deduction are incredible, Dip.*'

'*Just get in there, and let's see what we can disrupt.*'

The door was locked. Daisy groaned, and then felt under the flame-haired wig for her own silver hair, and pulled out a hairpin.

'*Really?*' whispered Sarah.

'*Just remember, the old ways are often the best.*'

In thirty seconds the lock was in their way no more. They filed inside the engine room, and Celia closed the door behind them. They were alone, and for the moment, safe from prying eyes.

The engine room was big, and more than just an engine room. In front of them were huge battery boxes, together with the electronic wizardry that distributed power to everywhere on the ship.

They could hear the sound of something running. Aidan pointed over to one side wall, where banks of dials and switches were relaying constant information to crewmembers who weren't there right then. Next to the monitoring cabinets was a generator, cocooned in a sound-box to kill much of the noise of it running constantly.

Next to that was a console, the screen above it blank, but ready for action when it was needed. Below the console were casings that looked like the guts of the computer which kept everything functioning.

'Can we shut that down?' said Daisy. 'I can stick my sword in it.'

Aidan shook his head. 'Maybe not a good idea, dear. If that computer controls all systems, gutting it will likely kill everything... including stuff we might need to help save our lives. We need to disrupt the bad guys, not put ourselves at risk.'

'You're being too sensible again, dear. So what can I stick my sword into?'

'Guys?' Sarah called out. She was on the far side of the room, looking at something sitting on a bench, covered by a blanket.

They walked over to join her. Daisy narrowed her eyes. 'So it's a mortuary as well.'

The human-shaped lump under the blanket wasn't exactly a joyous find. Aidan lifted back the top of the blanket. It was obvious what was hidden from sight underneath it, but as the grey, lifeless face met their gazes, Celia let out a shuddery kind of cry.

Aidan pulled her to him. 'Well, I guess the victim's body had to be stored somewhere.'

'At least we can examine it now, see if there are any clues,' said Daisy, somewhat reluctantly.

Chapter 28

While Daisy and Sarah examined the gruesome body, Aidan and Celia explored the rest of the engine room. In the centre, the two big caterpillar diesels sat idle, side by side, connected to shafts that disappeared through the bottom of the boat, which clearly had propellers on their other ends.

'Kind of dispelling the pirate ship ambience,' mused Aidan.

'I guess it's rather like the Disney ride that started it all. Giving the impression of stepping back into another era, but controlled by state-of-the art electronics.'

'Shame those safety protocols don't exist here right now,' he grinned.

'Well they do. They've just been switched off.'

Aidan glanced to a workbench built along the side of the hull. 'Talking of switching things off...'

Sitting on the bench was a small box, which didn't look like it was supposed to belong anywhere. A single green light was gently flashing away, a cable running to an electrical socket feeding it power.

'I think this might be the signal jammer.'

Daisy appeared next to them. 'Yes, it is. It's similar to one MI6 used back in Afghanistan, to prevent terrorists detonating bombs via mobile phone signals. Just a more modern version.'

'You find any clues on the body, dear?'

'Not really. There's no sign of death prior to hanging. The poor man must have been hauled up there to die from a rope around his neck.'

'*Euww...*' said Celia.

'Yes, dear. I think I'd rather walk the plank.'

'So no clues as to who did it then?'

Sarah cast her eyes desolately to the ceiling. 'Not one. Without sophisticated forensic equipment we can't even see if there are any fingerprints on him. And by the time we get him off this ship, if we ever do, he'll be too decomposed to get any firm prints.'

'Bugger.'

'Yes, bugger indeed, dear.' Daisy glanced at the engines. 'Those are big diesels, Dip.'

'There's a lot of weight in this ship to move through the water. They need to be sizeable.'

She walked over to the workbench, looked deep in thought. 'Correct me if I'm wrong, but it's my thinking these beasties will be called into action soon.'

'What are you saying, mum?'

Daisy picked up an adjustable spanner from the bench. 'It seems to me we can't be lying very far from Blackwater Bay. They've furled the sails, and I can't imagine they'd bother to unfurl them just to travel a mile or so. So my guess is they'll use these engines.'

'I still don't see how that helps us, dear.'

'You're the mechanical genius, Dip. Am I right in thinking diesel engines don't like running without oil in the sumps?'

'They'll seize up really quickly... ah, now I see the thinking.'

'Well I don't,' said Celia. 'How's that going to help anything?'

'First off, if the bad guys set off for home but don't get there, they'll have a distraction trying to figure out why the engines have clunked to a stop. Second, with the jammer out of commission and everyone on board able to tell the world they're hostages, within a short while after that there'll be about a million rescuers arriving on the scene. And the mutineers are drifting helplessly. All at sea, you might say.'

'They could still start killing people.'

'Maybe. But if you're surrounded by the enemy with no way out, why make things worse for yourself?'

'I suppose if you discovered the jammer is defunct, and then the engines are too, and the enemy are closing in on all sides...'

'And a few of the hostages are fighting back...'

'Yes, dear. If you're Dimitri in the middle of all that, and you've got rather a lot to worry about, the last thing you're going to do is start slaughtering hostages.'

Daisy lowered her head. 'It's a calculated risk, guys. But it might be the only one we have. Sarah, can you let Burrows know right now what we're doing, so he can start mustering the troops?'

She nodded, slipped the earpiece in and spoke into the microphone. Daisy looked at Aidan, waggled the spanner at him. 'Can you get the oil out of the sumps, Dip?'

'There should be drain plugs.' He glanced to the hull underneath the engines. 'And it's regulations to have sump trays to catch the oil if it leaks, so that'll work... as long as no one comes down here and notices the trays are full.'

'We'll have to chance that. Not likely though; the engines will surely be controlled from the same place as the ship's wheel on the quarterdeck, so hopefully no one will need to come in here.'

'Yes, the very modern starter and throttle controls are hidden behind a false front on the binnacle, so they're only seen when the engines are being used. I noticed someone checking them over just before we left Yarmouth.'

168

'Good. Get to work with your trusty spanner then, dear. Cella and me will deal with the jammer.'

Daisy and her daughter walked over to the device, as Aidan ripped off his colourful Calico Jack shirt and slithered under the first diesel to find the sump plugs.

She looked at the small bit of technical wizardry. 'It looks so innocent. But it jams every mobile signal, even police bands.'

'Then how come it didn't stop Sarah's?'

'The device she smuggled aboard uses SSB waves, like walkie-talkies. Dimitri could have programmed the jammer to stop those too, but I'm guessing he didn't think that was necessary, and he's likely using an SSB band to liaise with his men on the shore anyway. But now it's got to be destroyed.'

Celia drew her mother's sword from her scabbard. 'I suppose just unplugging it won't be enough?' she said as she handed it to her, and unplugged the jammer anyway.

'Oh no... they'll soon come down to see what's wrong, plug it back in, and then notice all the engine oil in the trays instead of the sumps.'

'But when they realise it's not working, they'll come to investigate anyway.'

'Which is why we're going to wreck it and then leave it in the foyer. When they come to find out what's wrong, they won't need to go into the engine room to know.'

Celia grinned. 'You really do have a wicked side.'

'So I've been told.'

Aidan came up, pulling his shirt back on as he spoke. 'Plugs unscrewed. Oil spewing into the collector trays as I speak.'

Daisy grinned, wickedly. 'Always knew your mechanical expertise would come in handy one day, dear.'

169

'Excuse me..?'

Something stopped him saying any more. Daisy lifted the sword with both hands, and stabbed the point down hard onto the plastic casing of the jammer. It speared right in, and then just to make sure she stabbed it four more times.

'I think it's dead now,' she said in a satisfied kind of way.

Aidan was on the move. 'Ok, let's go, before someone wakes early and finds us here. I think we've done enough disrupting for one day, don't you?'

The others seemed to agree, followed him towards the door. They didn't quite make it. Someone else got there first, throwing it open from the foyer side, and grinning inanely at his discovery.

'Well, well, what have we here..?'

Chapter 29

'Jack Sparrow?'

'*Captain* Jack Sparrow, if you please.'

Daisy glared into the blackened eyes. 'The last time we saw you, you were rowing into the night for your freedom.'

'Ah. You saw that.'

'So are you a ghost now too?'

'Let us just say, dear lady, I omitted to take my personal stash of rum so came back for it, and leave it at that, shall we?'

Celia shook her head. 'So is it so hard to admit to yourself you do have a conscience after all, Jack?'

'Should you tell anyone, I will regretfully have to run my sword right through you.'

'Is this where I kiss you, and handcuff you to the deck rail instead?'

'All things considered, it might be best to face the Kraken rather than live with being a coward, Elizabeth.'

Daisy grinned. 'Welcome to the resistance, Jack.'

'With all due respect, I didn't actually say...'

Daisy showed him the defunct jammer under her arm. 'You can start by telling all the guests they can use their mobile devices now.'

'Yes, dear Anne, that is a positive step in the right direction.'

'Well, it solves one problem, hey captain?'

'Indeed. But it still doesn't solve the main problem.'

'No, but the main problem can be reduced by solving several little problems first, don't you think?'

'You may find solving the main problem is a bit of a problem though...'

'Will you stop with problems, please?' cried Celia. 'Perhaps the only problem here is your attitude to the problem, Jack?'

'Are you stealing my lines now?' he grinned, and then shook his head. 'Ok, so what do we do?'

'Right now, we get back to our cabins like nothing has happened. Then, when the guests wake and the mutineers start searching the rest of the cabins, please spread the word to those who haven't already realised they can use their phones now. Dimitri will soon discover he can't locate his treasure, and then I suspect he'll get everyone together and start threatening us as a last ditch attempt to find it.'

Aidan filled Jack in on what they'd been doing. 'As well as destroying the jammer, we've emptied the diesels of oil. So when he finally heads for land... well, he won't get very far. There'll be a flotilla of boats heading for us, and we'll be drifting helplessly. He'll have no way out.'

'But he might get desperate?'

'That's where we come in,' said Daisy. 'We'll have to make sure he and his men don't harm anyone. But I'm the only one with a working cutlass.'

Jack grinned. 'I know where there are three more very sharp swords.'

Aidan was on his wavelength straightaway. 'Barbossa's quarters. I saw them, displayed in a glass case.'

'Will Turner originals... well, someone from the eighteenth century anyway. They're kinda priceless... but they could be even more priceless in the next few hours.'

'Can you get them for us, Jack?'

'I am Captain Jack Sparrow, ma'am. I can maybe sneak in to his quarters when he gets everyone on deck for the final showdown, which he surely will.'

'Then, apart from defending the honour of the Black Pearl, that's your task. Are you with us?'

He grinned. 'Hell yeah. This is so exciting!'

'That's my line,' growled Sarah.

They closed the engine room door behind them, and Daisy locked it again with the magic hairpin. Then she placed the wrecked jammer right in front of it, so when they came to investigate why it wasn't working, they'd know straightaway it had been sabotaged, and someone was making a serious point by leaving it in clear sight.

There should be no need for anyone to bother entering the engine room.

They wished Jack all the best, and then slipped back into their respective rooms, undressed and sank under the duvets, like they'd never left their beds.

It was five in the morning, and through the gun-port window, the sky was just beginning to turn a faint shade of blue out to the east. It would likely be a couple of hours before the mutineers arrived to search their cabin.

Thanks to the mysterious Tia Dalma, they wouldn't find what they were looking for. But that brought its own problems. The hot-headed Dimitri wasn't going to be happy, and then discovering his jammer was suddenly unable to do its job would make his mood a hell of a lot worse.

There was no way to know how he would react, when push came to a huge shove. It would be up to Daisy and her resistance fighters to try and make sure no one came to harm.

But as she snuggled under the duvet and pulled Aidan close, she was acutely aware that when the sun came up on the new day, it would be their last one aboard the Black Pearl.

One way or another.

Chapter 30

It was six-thirty when someone hammered on the door. Neither Daisy nor Aidan had slept, both huddled together in bed waiting for the inevitable knock on the door. Aidan opened it, and immediately found himself roughly shoved aside.

'Get out of my way,' hissed a pirate with a Russian accent.

Daisy didn't think much of his attitude. 'Hey, thug. There's no need for that attitude.'

'Just shut your mouth, lady. If you know what is good for you.'

The man and the pirate accompanying him barged into the room. His mate headed straight for the en suite, and the unpleasant-looking Russian ripped the bedclothes off the mattress, then looked under it, swore like he was under serious pressure to find the treasure, and then ripped out drawers and emptied the contents onto the mattress.

The other thug came back from the en suite. 'Nothing there,' he said gruffly, and then began helping his mate ransack the room. The pillows were ripped apart, and the floor began to look like a war zone, so much stuff slung over it.

Then they saw the scabbards which Daisy and Aidan had deliberately left in full view, slid out the swords and tipped them upside down.

Daisy glanced to Aidan, saw him let out an almost-imperceptible nod of relief that Tia Dalma had intervened. Then she had something else to think about, as the intruder began to feel her all over.

'Touch my boobs and I'll rip your head off,' she growled to the man, who touched them anyway, and then told her she was trying his patience. Then he ripped off the wig, just to make sure the treasure wasn't hidden underneath.

'I must complain to the management about the service in this hotel,' she said, trying his patience even further. He raised his hand to make sure she knew just how much she was pissing him off, but the other guy grabbed his wrist. 'Leave it, Sergei. There's nothing here.'

He'd finished examining Aidan, who was looking a little flustered at the intrusion, but was about to intervene if the other guy hadn't got there first.

Sergei lowered his hand. *'Think yourself lucky, old woman,'* he hissed as he followed his mate to the door.

'I'll still be making an official complaint...' Daisy called after him, unable to resist the retort.

Aidan slapped a hand over her mouth, but the men were already through the door, slamming it after them so hard the wooden walls shook.

Daisy replaced the wig. 'Well, that was an experience, dear,' she said, in a slightly shaky voice.

'Not one I care to ever go through again,' he said, pulling her close.

'At least they didn't discover my sword wasn't fake.'

He wiped the single tear from her eyes. 'I guess what just happened makes you even more determined to use it now.'

'You bet. It won't be just the sharp end of my tongue that Sergei feels next time.'

'Sadly dear, that may well come to pass before this is over.'

They looked around at the devastation ten minutes of ransacking had done. Nothing was where it was supposed to be, hardly a square foot of floor visible between the things that shouldn't be there.

'Come on, dear. Let's do the housework,' Daisy said with a faltering sigh.

They made a start on replacing drawers, and then Celia and Sarah arrived, gave them both consoling hugs, and lent a helping hand to put things back where they belonged.

'That Russian thug felt me up,' Daisy growled. 'And I don't think he was a doctor looking for lumps.'

'Oh, he was looking for a lump alright. Just one that wasn't part of you,' said Celia.

'Yes, well... the first chance I get he won't have the hands he should have kept to himself.'

The cabin looked like it did before the ransacking. Aidan brewed coffees, and they sipped the brew, listening to the sounds of searching and protesting coming from the next cabin.

It made painful listening, all of them knowing Sergei and his mate were leaving no stone unturned, human or otherwise. Daisy's fists clenched and unclenched, until Aidan took her wrist, and made a point of directing his gaze onto her hands, telling her without words that she was expressing her disgust without even realising she was.

'After that cabin there are only two others, and that's it. Once they realise it's not anywhere, that's when Dimitri will start to get desperate. About another half an hour, I estimate.'

'You think they've found the jammer yet?'

'I don't know. If they haven't, it won't be long. The galley staff will surely be going on duty any time now. They'll see it in the foyer straightaway.'

'But I don't think any of them are in Dimitri's gang of mutineers. If they realise what it is, they might hide it for a while.'

'Maybe,' said Sarah. 'But it's not obvious what it does to anyone who doesn't know. They might think it's some sort of bomb.'

Aidan nodded. 'If they do, someone will inform Dimitri. Which coincidentally, might be just about the time he is told they can't find the Crimson Heart.'

'Oh, the poor man,' said Daisy sarcastically. 'Life on the ocean wave won't be very jolly for him if both those things happen around the same time.'

'Or for us,' pointed out Celia.

That kind of killed the conversation. She'd made a very good point. Sarah had been in touch with Burrows, who had organised a small flotilla of police and coastguard boats that were lying a mile away out of sight, but ready to intercept the Black Pearl as soon as she gave the word. Both he and Sarah knew they had no choice but to wait for the right moment.

Moving too soon, while Dimitri still believed the Crimson Heart was being hidden by one of the guests, would for sure result in a last-gasp bloodbath. Once he knew his mutiny had definitely failed, he would be much more focussed on just escaping with his life.

Which might spare the lives of the guests.

Sarah had told Daisy of the plan, which was hardly ideal, but with so many hostages it was all they had to work with. Daisy nodded her head in agreement, but told herself silently Dimitri escaping with his life was something that went against her personal grain.

He'd put her family in mortal danger, and that couldn't be forgiven. If she got the chance to stop him escaping without getting into trouble herself, she'd make sure he never got away. In any shape or form.

She found her hand inadvertently gripping the hilt of the sword in her scabbard, took it away before anyone noticed, and forced a smile.

'Any which way, I think sometime in the next hour the peace and quiet will be shattered. Be ready, guys,' she said.

Chapter 31

Daisy's prediction was, unfortunately, right. It was just a half-hour later when the sounds coming from the corridor told them the action was starting.

The coarse shouts of the mutineer pirates were accompanied by the terrified cries of the guests, who were being forced out of their cabins. A minute later their door burst open, and the vision of loveliness which was the thoroughly-unpleasant Sergei was framed in the doorway, brandishing his sword menacingly to them.

'On deck, all of you... now,' he growled.

The four of them filed out of the room, joined some of the other guests in the crowded corridor. They already knew what was happening, and it looked like most of the other guests had worked it out too, the frightened expressions on their faces and the sobs of a few of the women confirming it.

The final showdown had started, and they were about to face the wrath of a very unhappy Davy Jones.

An early-morning sun had just cleared the low hills to the east as they made the main deck. Straightaway Daisy saw Dimitri pacing impatiently up and down, waiting for his hostages to assemble, his evil stubbly face set in a grim expression.

Daisy smiled to herself as she saw his demeanour, knowing he was feeling like a failed treasure-hunter right then. Her smile was as grim as his though, tempered by the harsh fact the man was likely to try something desperate, a last-ditch attempt to make sure he hadn't failed yet again.

Five of his mutineer crew were waving their swords menacingly at the guests as they assembled nervously into a huddled group. There was no sign of Jack Sparrow or Will Turner.

'*I can't see Will,*' Celia whispered, as she slipped a shaking hand into her mother's.

'Oh, he'll be around somewhere. If what you told me is true, he'll not want any part of what might happen next, if he can avoid it.'

Daisy glanced across the estuary. There was no sign of the waterborne cavalry, who were keeping well out of sight until the Black Pearl raised anchor and headed for Blackwater Bay, and Sarah gave the word to move in.

It was just too risky to the hostages for the cavalry to make their move right then. While Dimitri still believed there was a chance of finding his treasure, he held all the cards. Once he knew he was never going to find it, the tables would turn.

That was when the British soldiers could move in.

Sarah leant her face close to Daisy's. Her earpiece was in place, hidden by her blonde hair. '*I don't like this, Daisy. He looks evil. What if he starts killing hostages?*'

'*I don't think he'll actually kill anyone. But he'll threaten to. If it comes to it, we'll have to defend them, and you'll have to give the word.*'

'*You're the only one with a working sword right now, remember?*'

'*Not forgotten. We'll have to rely on Jack Sparrow to change that when he can.*'

'*Are you listening to yourself? The so-called man who rowed away for his life last night?*'

'*He came back, didn't he?*'

'*Sometimes I wish I had your faith.*'

'Hope, dear. Hope.'

Their whispered conversation was interrupted. The frightened murmurings of the other guests faded away as Dimitri's voice boomed out across the deck.

'You will be aware you are here because we have failed in our quest to recover the treasure. Our time is about to expire, and so you have left me little choice. First of all I will ask you all *nicely*... whichever one of you has cleverly concealed the pendant from us, hand it over right now.'

Daisy, fired up by the stubble on his face and the dark evil in his eyes, couldn't resist calling out. 'Give it up, Dimitri. You've failed yet again. Just get lost and leave these people alone.'

It maybe wasn't Daisy's best move. He strode over to her, the black boots clunking menacingly on the deck planks. 'So, Miss Bonny, what makes you so sure I will not succeed?'

She swallowed hard. He did make a formidable, and unpredictable sight. She met his stare defiantly. 'Because it obviously isn't here. Your men abused everyone and their possessions trying to find it, and you killed Barbossa for nothing. In my book that makes you a dismal failure.'

A big hand flew swiftly, smacking into the side of Daisy's face, sending her staggering back a step or two. Aidan began to move forward, intend on retaliating for the blow, but Celia pulled him back.

'Leave it, dad. He's got a sharper sword than you.'

He shook his head, but knew his daughter was right. Starting a full-scale fight right then would inevitably result in innocent blood being spilled.

Dimitri looked more evil than ever. His mouth twitching with his fury, he just about managed to get the words out. 'You call me a dismal failure, Anne Bonny? When it was you

181

who ended up in Port Royal prison under sentence of death?'

Daisy rubbed her stinging cheek, but still held his stare, even though she would rather not have. 'You're mixing fantasy and reality, Dimitri. And anyway, I escaped, didn't I? And here I am now, being a pain in your neck, you murdering piece of Russian crap .'

He wasn't getting any calmer. '*Murderer?* You think I killed Barbossa?'

'Actually, yes.'

The fist lifted into the air again. It didn't land. Someone caught his arm, stopped him landing the blow. 'Pardon my intrusion, captain sir. But it was you who said time was running out. Perhaps we should concentrate our efforts on the matter in hand?' said the more sensible Mr. Gibbs.

Dimitri growled out his intense frustration. But the fist lowered, and he stomped away a few paces, and then turned and addressed his guests.

'As you see, my patience is wearing thin. So here is the deal. Whoever has the treasure, hand it over now. If you do not, in five minutes time we will begin killing you, one by one, and will not stop until whoever has it gives it up. Decide if jewels are more important than human life, all of you.'

Daisy shook her head, slipped her hand into Aidan's. 'Well that's ironic, considering he's already decided treasure is more important than life itself.'

'Other people's lives anyway,' Sarah pointed out.

'Ok, all of you. I don't think he'll actually kill anyone, but given the state of him right now, I can't be certain. Be ready for instant action, guys.'

Then, something happened to make Dimitri Novalenko's mood even darker. And answer the question on Celia's mind. Suddenly they knew where Will Turner was. He appeared at the top of the staircase, carrying something in his arms.

Something that looked suspiciously like a signal jammer, with five mortal wounds in its casing.

Chapter 32

Will deliberately placed the defunct jammer at Dimitri's feet, without a word. He didn't really need to say anything. For ten seconds the mutineer captain stared at it in disbelief, his fists clenching and unclenching with fury.

Then he sprang into action, roared like a cornered lion, picked it up and threw it over the side.

'Anne Bonny... you devious bitch...' he screamed as it hit the water, and moments later, sank without trace.

'Hey... why do I get the blame for everything around here?'

'What? First you stab my mask to death, then you call me a murderer, now you kill my signal jammer? And you wonder why I blame you for everything?'

'Well, if you put it like that...'

'How long have you all had signal back?' he shrieked to the guests.

Aidan couldn't resist a slightly-wicked grin. 'Oh, about three hours now, Davy.'

'How...' He strode up to Daisy, lifting his cutlass from its scabbard. 'Perhaps this time round, Miss Bonny, you will not manage to escape.'

Daisy drew her sword, held it at an angle in front of her face. 'So I'm right after all. You are a murderer... not that you'll actually get the chance to kill anyone else.'

The crowd of guests backed away, as far as they could in the confines of the main deck. And once again the two enemies squared up to each other. Aidan glanced to Sarah. There was little he could do with a pretend sword, and there was still no sign of Jack with anything sharper. Five of the loyal mutineers had drawn their very real swords, waiting for instructions from their captain, who right then was somewhat otherwise occupied.

The two opponents clashed swords, just the once, and then both backed away a little, bracing themselves for a full-on attack.

But then something happened to halt everyone in their tracks. From above their heads, a voice called out.

'Stop!'

A figure stood on the edge of the quarterdeck, eight feet above them. She smiled confidently, showing the vegetable-dye-blackened teeth. She'd silenced the deck, everyone staring like statues at the strange woman looking down on them.

She spoke again, her voice seeming to boom out in the early-morning silence. 'So, Davy Jones, ye am a dismal failure for sure.'

He stared at her like life couldn't get any more bizarre. But at least he found a hiss or two. 'Don't you dare insult me. Where the hell did you come from, anyway?'

'Me am a ghost. Ye not know of me?'

'You... you're Tia... something-or-other...'

'Me Tia Dalma, voodoo sorceress. And ye is cursed, and always will be.'

'Oh, come on. Russians do not believe in that crap. Any Russian who isn't a peasant at least.'

'Ye should believe, foolish man. Ye have not found treasure, and ye am on the edge of reason. And still you tink ye is not cursed?'

Dimitri glanced to his men. 'Someone go and run that woman through, before I lose patience altogether.'

Sergei and another mutineer headed for the steps, but Tia had other plans.

'Wait! It be yet another foolish move, sea dog. Then you will *never* find the treasure ye seek.'

'What? What are you saying, you crazy freak?'

Tia's hands went to her neck, and eased out a silver chain from behind her beads. Then she pulled the Crimson Heart from her neck, and dangled it in front of her. 'Is dis what ye seek, Davy Jones?'

A gasping murmur drifted from the crowd. Dimitri's face creased into a rare smile. He waved his men away from the steps, beamed lovingly to Tia.

'I knew it was on this ship.'

'Ye is such a clever man, Davy. So, do ye want it?'

'More than anything,' he breathed.

'So what ye prepared to sacrifice to have what ye desire?'

'Excuse me..?'

'Untold riches always come with a price, Davy Jones. Ye of all people should know that.'

'So... what do you want?'

'For ye to let every one of these people go, unharmed.'

'I... I can't do that,' he stammered, knowing if he let them all go he'd never escape. 'I have to keep a few of them hostage, as my insurance policy. I... I'll let the rest of them go, I promise.'

'Not good enough, Davy. Ye release dem all, or ye do not get the treasure.'

'Are you holding *me* to ransom now? Remember, I'm the one with the swords, and you appear to be unarmed.'

'Perhaps. But me hold the biggest weapon of all, does me not?'

'Sure. And I can take it off you, just like that.'

'Ye sure, dog?'

186

Dimitri nodded to Sergei and the other man, who set off up the steps again. 'Oh yeah, I'm sure.'

Tia moved a foot to her right, so she was pressed up against the upper deck rail. 'Then you am still foolish.'

She held her arm out over the side of the boat, the pendant dangling from an outstretched finger. 'Me suggest ye call off yur monkeys, Davy Jones.'

Sergei hesitated, almost at the top of the steps. Dimitri waved him away again, the last thing he really wanted to do. Sergei and his equally-unpleasant mate dropped back to the main deck.

'Ok, Tia. That is delightfully amusing, but you would never drop something so valuable over the side. So can we stop this nonsense and cut a deal, please?'

She raised her eyes like she was shocked by his words, but the Crimson Heart stayed in its perilous position. 'So Davy Jones, ye have been cursed once before, but still ye do not believe in tings ye have already experienced?'

'Shall we stop the pretence, whoever you are? It's all peasant nonsense, as you are aware. Please... please just pull your arm back in, and let's make a deal. *Please?'*

She laughed. 'So now once more ye are helpless. Ye tink I make deal with man who is cursed?'

'I said stop it.'

'And me said all them hostages go free, or ye will never see the treasure again.'

Dimitri looked like he was at the biggest fork in the road he'd ever known. 'Look, Tia. Let us be reasonable. By now the authorities will know what's going on here. How can I return the Crimson Heart to its rightful ownership if I can't take a few hostages to help me escape?'

187

Tia sneered. *'Rightful ownership?* A Russian mafia family who actually stole it? You tink your family am rightful owners?'

'Well, you know what I mean.'

'Ye is *all* cursed.'

Dimitri threw his hands in the air, knowing time really was running out. 'I am getting tired of talk of curses. Please come down here, and let us celebrate our good fortune over vodka.'

Daisy glanced to Aidan. 'I don't think I need to be a voodoo sorceress to know what happens next, do I dear?'

'I don't tink you do, no,' he grinned.

'Just be ready for all hell to break loose.'

Tia was shaking her head. 'Me will never drink with ye, thief. Us has little in common, apart from killing people.'

Dimitri visibly gulped. He also knew what was possibly about to happen. He held out a begging hand. *'Tia, please...'*

She gazed fondly at the pendant swinging gently from her finger. 'Metinks dis is so terribly cursed, there can be only one place it belong.'

Dimitri gasped. *'No...'*

Tia looked back to him, and for a moment their gazes met.

And then what was always going to happen, happened.

'Oops,' she said.

Chapter 33

A gasp of disbelief wafted through the watching crowd as the plop of the Crimson Heart hitting the water filled the still morning air. Dimitri gasped too, somewhat louder, stood rooted to the spot for a moment, and then rushed to the deck rail and stared over the side at the place where the ripples were fanning out with depressing finality.

'Get after it...' he croaked to his men, who looked at each other like they couldn't quite believe what they were hearing.

Mr. Gibbs pointed out what was blatantly obvious. 'Captain, that treasure is heavy, and it sure ain't gonna float. It be just about to hit the sea bed any second.'

Dimitri screamed his fury, stamped a booted foot onto the deck to make sure everyone knew just how bad he was feeling. Then he buried his face in his hands, as realisation dawned his search was finally over.

And just as Daisy had predicted, his thoughts went straight to plan B.

'Get those engines running. Head for the rendezvous, full speed!'

'Full speed?' Aidan gulped. 'Those engines won't last long at all, at that speed.'

Dimitri ran up the steps to the quarterdeck, intent on doing Tia Dalma irreparable harm. Then his head flicked from side to side at manic speed. She was nowhere to be seen. Like the ghost she told him she was, she was gone.

'Where the hell...'

Mr. Gibbs had followed him. 'Might I suggest we leave retribution for another time, captain? Perhaps running for freedom is more important right now?'

189

He pulled the false capping off the binnacle as he spoke, turned the keys to start the engines. The small crowd on the deck felt the vibrations as the diesels burst into life, and then they heard the rattle of the anchor chain as it was hastily winched up.

Mr. Gibbs didn't give the engines any warm-up time, threw both throttles to full, and the ship began to move forward. In seconds it was travelling faster than it had ever gone before. He spun the wheel, and the Black Pearl headed further along the estuary, in the direction of Blackwater Bay, a couple of miles distant.

Dimitri clutched his hands to his cropped head, feeling his world crumbling around his feet. What he didn't know was that things were even worse that he thought. As he whipped out his SBB communicator and spoke to his men waiting in the trees surrounding the bay, neither he nor them were aware that, thanks to Daisy's eavesdropping, a SWAT unit was already hiding there, waiting for the word to move in.

And, just to put a final lid on his day, the Black Pearl was now heading *towards* the fleet of police boats, hidden just out of sight around the next wide bend.

But Dimitri wasn't finished attempting to escape the clutches of the law. He'd done it a few times before, and he forced himself to believe he could do it again.

He ran back down the steps to the main deck, to where his men were waiting nervously for his instructions. *'Be ready,'* he barked to them, and then stomped over to Daisy. 'You, you interfering old woman. You're responsible for this. What have you got to say for yourself?'

She faced him up, the sword still in her hand. 'First, if you call me old again, I'll run you through. Second, unless

190

you've forgotten already, I wasn't the one who dumped the treasure overboard.'

For a moment he looked lost for words, but then glared an evil stare into her. 'I have no doubt you had something to do with... everything.'

'I had no idea Tia Dalma was going to do that,' she said, truthfully.

He screamed his frustration, turned away, and stomped back over to his men. 'Grab five women as insurance. When we get to the rendezvous, they come with us until we're safely away.'

The mutineers headed for the crowd, but then Daisy put herself in their way. 'Take anyone hostage, and you'll be sorry.'

She braced her sword, halting them in their tracks. They looked to their captain, unsure what to do. He shook his head and sneered, confident he still had the upper hand... when it came to escaping at least.

'Are you that lily-livered, men? An old woman making you tremble? *Kill her!*'

Daisy gave him the glare. 'I told you what would happen if you called me old again. But right now, this one's nearer...'

She lunged the cutlass at the closest mutineer, sliced a chunk of his shirt, and a little skin beneath it. It happened to be Sergei, who didn't look too amused at being taken by surprise. As Daisy backed away, he raised his sword to retaliate, growling out his displeasure. *'I'm going to enjoy this, Bonny...'*

'Cease!' Dimitri finally saw the bigger picture, and realised spilling pointless blood on the deck wasn't going to help his cause. 'Take her sword, and move her aside.'

Daisy relaxed, allowed Sergei to take the sword, knowing right then she was well outnumbered. And aware they'd been under way for five minutes, and that the engines weren't going to last much longer.

'Where's that Jack Sparrow?' Celia whispered.

'There...' said Daisy quietly, spotting him lurking furtively against the forecastle wall, waiting for a distraction so he could sneak into Barbossa's quarters and pinch the swords without anyone noticing.

Daisy gave him one. As Sergei and another mutineer tended to his wounds, she snatched her sword back, and cried out the first thing that came to mind.

'Avast, ye lubbers!'

As she swished her weapon in a slightly out-of-control half circle, the mutineers stepped back a little. Whether they were more shocked by her actions or her words, it wasn't clear. But she'd achieved her objective... Dimitri and his men had all their eyes on the crazy woman with the sword.

As Jack seized the moment and slipped inside Barbossa's quarters, she swung the weapon again.

'Any of ye man enough to take me on?'

The mutineers seemed to think they were, lining up to take her down. She'd backed herself into an intentional corner, and suddenly things weren't looking too good. But then something else happened, and took some of the distraction duties away from her.

From somewhere below them, ominous-sounding grating noises were accompanied by just as ominously big vibrations. For ten seconds everything seemed to get worse, and then the engines let out a final loud clunky kind of bang, and gave up completely.

Daisy tried to keep the smile from her face, but it wasn't easy. Aidan's intervention could not have produced the desired effect at a better time. She felt him slip a hand into hers, glanced into his eyes and saw the fear in them.

'Well that worked perfectly, dear,' he said quietly. 'But I worry about what happens next. Someone isn't going to be too pleased.'

None of them knew it, but the desired effect had been perhaps a little too dramatic. Aidan wasn't a marine engineer, and had no idea the reduction gearboxes between the engines and the shafts used the same oil as the engines. One of them had simply given up the ghost along with its engine. The other one had behaved a little more extravagantly.

The overheated gearbox had shattered, propelling one gear wheel right off its spindle, and right through the thin aluminium casing.

And then, straight through the bottom of the boat.

Chapter 34

'Now?' said Sarah to Daisy.

'That might be prudent, dear,' Daisy nodded.

Sarah pulled the mike from behind her hair. *'Go go go, sir,'* she said.

'On our way, Lowry. Be five minutes though. Can you guys stop any carnage until then?'

'Do our best, sir.'

Daisy glanced around, taking stock. The mutineer crew were looking like they didn't know what to do next. Dimitri was still stomping around, shouting to no one in particular to find out why they were now drifting helplessly towards the shore.

Then it seemed to dawn on him how perilous his situation was. *'Grab some women...'* he shrieked to his confused crew.

Sergei and a few others started to move towards the guests. Then Jack Sparrow was there, throwing swords to Aidan, Sarah and Celia. Aidan looked at the weapon in his hand.

'Wow, this is one beautiful piece of kit...'

'Dear..?' cried Daisy. 'Really, now?'

He shook his head, suddenly aware of why the beautiful piece of kit was in his hand. Daisy raised her sword at the mutineers. 'I've told you, touch any of the women and you'll be sorry!'

The four crewmembers came to a halt, turned to look disbelievingly at Daisy instead. Sergei grinned venomously. 'You're like a snappy mongrel terrier, old woman. You really think you and your motley crew can stop us?'

She and Aidan positioned themselves between the mutineers and the guests. 'Maybe, maybe not. Regardless, not all of us will come out of it in one piece,' Daisy growled, swinging the sword violently to make a point.

Dimitri, a few feet behind his men, realised time was rapidly running out. He screamed to his pirates, in a slightly-higher-pitched voice than normal. *'Get the women... now. We have to go.'*

All hell broke loose. The mutineers, led by a desperate Sergei, advanced on the frightened guests once more. The clash of swords filled the air, as Daisy and Aidan stood their ground. Sarah joined them, and it became three against four.

Celia looked at the sword in her hands, and then at her parents thrusting and parrying for their lives. For a second she wondered if she'd somehow fallen into a drug-induced dream, then cast her eyes to the sky and decided that even if she had, Elizabeth Swann would have the spirit to do the right thing.

She joined the fray, slashing wildly at the mutineers. Now it was four against four. No one had time to look, but a small flotilla of police boats had just appeared around the bend, less than a mile away.

Jack Sparrow fought his way towards the rear of the deck, whipped the tarpaulins off the lifeboats, and attached the lifting ropes to the ancient-looking but state-of-the-art hydraulic swinging crane. He shouted to the guests above the noise of the clashing swords, as the first lifeboat swung over the side. *'Get in... I'll lower you down...'*

The guests rushed to scramble in, but someone with a bit of sound thinking organised them a little. There were only two boats, the third already in the water, tied to the rear of the ship after Jack had made his escape and then changed his mind. Designed to hold twenty people each, there was just enough capacity for the guests... if they somehow remained calm.

He began to lower the first boat, watched as it met the water, a little before he expected it to. In Jack Sparrow fashion, he voiced his concern out load to himself.

'If what's going on around me isn't concerning enough, does it appear we're not as far above the surface as we used to be?'

As someone in the lifeboat detached the lifting ropes, and he grabbed them back and fastened them to the second boat and swung that over the side, he could see his musings were correct. They definitely weren't as far above the surface as they should be... and not even as far as they were two minutes ago.

The mutineers were slowly forcing Daisy and her defenders back. She managed to throw a quick glance to the estuary, saw the cavalry about half a mile away. Unfortunately Dimitri saw it too, and realised his time really was up. He drew his sword, desperate to grab at least a couple of hostages to be sure of his escape.

Daisy also saw what Jack had seen. The Black Pearl was considerably lower in the water. She screamed to Aidan, as she parried a vicious lunge from an increasingly-frantic mutineer.

'What the hell did you do, dear? Correct me if I'm wrong, but we appear to be sinking!'

He cast a quick glance to the water. 'Um... we are sinking, Flower. But all I did was remove the oil...'

A breathless Celia cried out, 'When you said scupper the ship, I didn't think you meant it literally...'

Daisy had no time to reply. Dimitri was standing right in front of her, an evil look on his face. He raised his sword. *'Get out of my way, old woman...'*

She knew what he was thinking. The last of his hostages were already climbing into the second boat. He had no way of escaping other than to grab a couple of them before they were gone, and then use the third boat tied at the stern to get to the rendezvous, and escape with his insurance policy.

She and her defenders had to stop him reaching the guests. Now he'd joined the fray, they were slightly outnumbered once again. And something else had been added to the mix.

The cavalry was speeding towards them, but was still two or three minutes away. The drifting Black Pearl was being carried by the wind, blowing it right to Blackwater Bay. The tiny cove was less than half a mile away. If Dimitri was able to grab a couple of women and reach the lifeboat, he might only have to row a few yards, and then be on dry land. With his get-out-of-jail-free card.

Daisy knew that come what may, they had to stop him getting to the hostages.

Chapter 35

Suddenly, it was five-a-side once more. A flash of brown and white landed next to Celia, the sword in his hand already slashing at the mutineers.

'Will,' she gasped, a smile breaking over her face.

'I told you I would defend you, Elizabeth,' he grinned, parrying a thrust from an enemy sword as he spoke.

Dimitri had no intention of taking prisoners. Like a demon possessed, he slashed away at Daisy, forcing her back to the main deck rail. His sheer determined commitment to escape had taken her by surprise. Aidan was too engrossed with his own opponent to help. So was everyone else, stuck in one-to-one combat.

Desperately she parried his crazed thrusts, knowing his only desire right then was to end her life and grab his insurance policy before it disappeared. Daisy was growing tired, and growing more aware she was being outfought. Just one thrust she couldn't avoid, and it would be over...

Jack Sparrow saw the mutineers getting closer to the last boat, which he's just begun lowering to the water. He groaned to himself. Daisy looked like she was about to succumb to Dimitri's insane attack. The water was rising as the ship sank lower in the water, but it was touch and go whether the mutineers could overcome their opponents, and if Dimitri would reach the lifeboat before it made the surface.

He had to do something to protect the hostages, and help the resistance.

What would the real Jack Sparrow do?

He shouted to the people in the boat. *'Enjoy the water-splash ride!'* Then he slashed his sword at the ropes lowering it down. It was less than a ten foot drop, the Black Pearl already way lower in the water than it should be. But as the lifeboat plummeted the final part of its journey, with all the weight in it, it still made a big, loud splash.

Big enough to distract Dimitri from his crazed attack on Daisy. As he glanced round and realised his insurance policy had finally run out, he screamed a blood-curdling cry. Jack stepped back down to the main deck, and joined Daisy as she suddenly found new energy, and swung her sword at the Russian again.

And then Dimitri's day got a little bit worse. From two hundred yards across the water, Burrow's voice coming through a loud-hailer was the last thing he needed to hear.

'Dimitri Novalenko and the mutineers, stand down. It's over. Drop your weapons.'

He swore, several times, in Russian. For a second his sword dropped to his side, and Daisy's wicked grin was all he could see. But then his instinct for survival kicked in.

He bolted.

The fighting wasn't over. As the sound of still-clashing swords filled Daisy's ears, she spun around. Three of the mutineers had finally realised fighting for a pay-day that was gone was pointless, done as they were told and dropped their swords. But Dimitri's right-hand man Sergei was Russian too.

And in his world, it wasn't over until it was over.

He snarled his defiance, and took everyone by surprise. Celia had also lowered her sword, thinking the battle was over. But Sergei's desperate need for retribution wasn't done. He lunged at Celia, knowing she was the daughter of the woman who had ruined everything... and drawn his blood as well, adding injury to insult.

Celia realised just in time he was still bent on revenge, arched her body to avoid the tip of the blade. She couldn't go any further, backed against the deck rail. Sergei raised his sword for a final slash, knowing Celia was an open target.

Then Will was there, using his body to shield her. He slashed out at Sergei, who ducked, but then the Russian seized his moment. Slightly off balance, Will was vulnerable for just half a second until he steadied himself.

It was a half-second too long.

Sergei's sword speared into his stomach, and as the blood began to stain his shirt, he crumpled to his knees, and let out a choking whisper.

'I'm so sorry, Elizabeth.'

As he lay flat on the deck at her feet, for a moment she could do nothing but stare disbelievingly at the man who'd run Will through. Then, as grappling hooks looped over the deck rail and officers began to climb aboard, she let out a desolate scream.

She lifted the sword at the grinning man who was just about to do the same to her, and as the tears poured down her face she swung at him, the force of a hundred emotions behind it. So violent and unexpected was her action, he had to stagger back to avoid getting slashed.

Daisy was right behind Sergei, running to do what she could to help her daughter. She was holding her sword at waist height, pointing out in front of her, ready to raise it and go back into battle.

She didn't get the chance.

Sergei, backing up, lost his balance slightly, and backed right into the point of Daisy's blade. As it sank through his lower back into his guts she cried out her shock, as surprised by what had happened as he was.

As he collapsed to the deck she pulled out the blade, let out a gasp as she saw the blood covering it. She was about to drop it in horror, but then a shout from Jack stopped her.

'Dimitri... he's getting away...'

Chapter 36

As Burrows and a posse of officers appeared over the deck rail, she sprang into action. Celia was standing like a statue, unable to move, staring at the awful sight of Will laying bleeding on the deck.

Two medics appeared, ran to Will, and started to rip his shirt away. Daisy felt a hand in hers, and for a second Aidan was there, making sure his wife was unharmed. Then she noticed Dimitri, heading up the steps to the quarterdeck.

Aidan spotted him too, saw Daisy's emotions ripped two ways. 'Go get him, Flower. I'll be there for Celia.'

She threw him a grateful smile, and ran after the Russian, who had just made the top of the steps. She knew where he was going; the lifeboat tied at the stern was his last slim hope of escape. Police boats were all around the Black Pearl, there was virtually no chance of him disappearing unnoticed.

Yet she knew he would still take that slim chance, come what may. And tiny though it was, she wasn't prepared to run the risk it would be successful.

Jack was already on the steps, followed by Sarah. Daisy clambered up, joined them on the raised quarterdeck. The Russian was already at the stern, looking down at the lifeboat twenty feet below him. The Black Pearl had drifted almost to the shore of Blackwater Bay. He could see freedom a hundred yards away.

The ship was almost scuppered. Daisy glanced back, saw the waves starting to lap over the low main deck. It looked like about a hundred officers were shuttling those still on board onto rescue boats. She felt a tear roll down her cheek as she saw Celia, refusing to leave Will, the paramedics lifting him clear of the water.

Then the ship shuddered. They'd stopped drifting, the waterlogged hull hitting a sandbank, two hundred feet from the shoreline. It wasn't going to sink any further. She heard the sound of helicopter blades beating the air, saw a speck of black and yellow in the distance. The emergency air ambulance was heading for them.

The cluster of police boats had moved to the middle section of the ship, concentrating on rescuing people. The much higher stern of the ship was devoid of life, apart from the three of them and the Russian gangster, standing there trying to decide if jumping for the lifeboat was a sensible course of action.

Sarah's sharp call thundered through the air. *'Dimitri Novalenko, give it up. There's no escape.'*

He glanced round, grinned insanely to her. 'Who are you to tell me what is what, when you were the one rescued from an almost impossible situation, hey?'

'Yeah well Dimitri, what you don't know is that I deliberately put myself in that situation, so you would save me. Officer Sarah Lowry at your service, here to effect your arrest.'

He shook his head as realisation finally dawned. 'So my men do a good deed, and end up suffering for it, yes?'

'Good deed?' I suppose taking forty hostages was a good deed too?'

Jack decided to be *Jack*. 'Take it from me, as one pirate to another. You need to know when the cannonballs are stacked too high against you, my friend.'

He didn't seem to appreciate that much. '*Hah*. Says you, who always manages to come up smelling of roses.'

'At least I don't come up smelling like the bottom of the sea, Davy Jones.' He took a step towards the Russian, who still had the sword in his hands.

'Don't come any closer, Jack... or you will find yourself losing your petals.'

'Please leave my personal bits out of this.'

'Still you play the fool, and make stupid jokes.'

'Just giving you something to think about, other than escaping, Dimitri.'

Dimitri glanced up, as yet another development gave him something else to think about. The air ambulance was hovering next to the stricken ship, a paramedic dropping from it with a rescue cradle.

The wind from the rotors was fanning a circle in the water, the noise from its engine all they could hear. Daisy glanced down to the main deck. Celia was crying, hanging desperately onto the cradle as the medics loaded Will onto it, her emotions getting the better of her.

Burrows pulled her away, said something she couldn't hear. Judging by her expression, it didn't seem to go down too well. Daisy's heart skipped a beat, her legs almost forcing themselves to go to her. Then she saw Aidan, wrapping his arms around their daughter, helping to lead her away as the medic signalled to the chopper, and the cradle began to rise into the air. Only a few people were left on deck, apart from Celia and Aidan, all of them service personnel.

Daisy turned away, unable to look any more at the sight of her distraught daughter. Then something snapped inside her. The man responsible for bringing her family so much pain was there, thirty feet away, about to take a leap of faith, and possibly get away with everything.

She lifted her bloodstained sword as she ran towards him, her mind incensed by the need for revenge, her emotions out of control. Someone called out her name urgently, she didn't even know if it was Sarah or Jack, her single-minded determination that Dimitri should pay for what he'd done the only thing on her mind.

He saw her coming, raised his sword to parry her vicious thrust. She could hear running footsteps on the deck behind her, but as she slashed wildly at the Russian again, nothing else mattered. He must have seen the crazed look in her eyes, and known the insane woman wasn't going to take no for an answer.

He was backed onto the stern of the ship, and Jack Sparrow and the police woman were advancing rapidly. He was all out of options.

Except one.

He slashed one last time at the woman who had ruined everything, forced her to back away a foot or two. It gave him just enough time to jump onto the deck rail, and launch himself feet first to the boat twenty feet below. A kamikaze scream reverberated through the air as Jack and Sarah reached Daisy, and the three of them hung over the side, just in time to see something that would be quite funny if it wasn't so unfunny.

Dimitri, still feet first, dropped into the boat at high speed. He missed the seat, instead plummeting straight to the rather thin fibreglass bottom of the hull. He wasn't exactly a light man, and falling from twenty feet up into a hull that wasn't designed for high-diving was only going to end one way.

He crashed right through the hull, into the sea below.

It didn't quite end there. The Black Pearl was beached on a sandbank, and there was only five feet of water below the lifeboat. As a stunned Dimitri felt his feet hit the bottom, and realised his head was still above water, surrounded by what was left of the lifeboat, he cried out his final agony.

And as the hull sank around him, he found some movement, stepped out of the wreckage, and began to swim for the shore.

Then Burrows was standing behind them, chuckling to himself in a mirthless way, pointing to the SWAT team who were running across the beach to welcome Dimitri Novalenko to Blackwater Bay.

'Guess he never stood a chance with you guys around,' he said.

Daisy sucked in a couple of breaths to bring her emotions back down. '*Will*... what's happening?'

Burrows lowered his head. 'The air ambulance is flying him to Addenbrookes. Celia is going with him. But he's lost a lot of blood. I'm afraid you might have to be prepared for the worst.'

Chapter 37

They made a strange sight, the infamous Anne Bonny, Calico Jack, and Elizabeth Swann sitting impatiently in the waiting room at Addenbrookes Hospital in Cambridge.

It was a very nice waiting room, with comfortable padded seats and large potted palms dotted around, and pictures of well-known Cambridge landmarks on the walls. But none of it could take away the dread in all of their hearts.

Daisy was fighting exhaustion, her head dropping onto Aidan's shoulder from time to time, as sleep got the better of her for a few moments, until she shook herself awake once more. Celia sat on her father's other side, her hand clasped firmly into his, her face giving away the fact her heart was doing its best not to break.

There was little conversation. There wasn't much anyone could say. There wasn't much any of them could do either, other than wait it out.

Burrows had told Sarah to drive Daisy and Aidan to the hospital, but she couldn't stay. The beached Black Pearl was a crime scene, and her boss wanted her back to help process the incident.

They'd arrived four hours ago, and found a distraught Celia sipping a polystyrene cup of coffee, which had gone stone cold a half-hour before they got there. Aidan had grabbed them all fresh drinks from the machine sitting on one wall, and Celia brought them up to speed with what little she knew.

Will had been rushed straight to surgery, and five hours later was still there. Three hours ago, a friendly nurse had told them he was in critical condition, but they were doing all they could, and someone would come to see them when he was out of theatre.

It was a busy day at Addenbrookes, a major road accident stretching the staff to their limits. It wasn't good timing for Will, and the staff nurse had been honest with Celia, told her his chances of pulling through were fifty-fifty at best.

Celia broke the depressed silence. 'How much longer, for god's sake? Just what are they doing to him?'

Aidan squeezed her hand a little tighter. 'Hold it together, dear. I'll go ask if there's any news, in case they've forgotten about us.'

She found a slight smile. 'Dressed like this? I doubt we're very forgettable right now.'

He smiled with her, walked over to the reception desk. A minute later he came back, lifting his hands from his sides. 'They don't know anything yet. He's still in surgery, along with three other critical patients. They're doing what they can, Celia.'

She shook her head, wiped away a tear. 'He could have chosen a quieter day to save my life...'

The words ended in a choky kind of sob. Daisy wrapped an arm around her daughter. 'Be strong, you. He'll come out the other side of this.'

'You don't know that.'

'Ok, he *deserves* to come out the other side.'

Aidan fetched more coffees, and the interminable wait started again. Nothing much else was said, all three of them knowing whatever words they spoke, they could never be the right ones.

Daisy's head flopped onto Aidan's shoulder once more, the rigours of sword-fighting to the death making it impossible to keep her eyes open, even though falling asleep was the last thing she wanted to do.

Then, something happened to take away the tendency to drift away. Aidan spotted her before the others; a junior nurse, walking hesitantly along the long corridor from the critical care wards. A distant figure at first, as she came nearer he could see a couple of clipboards in her hands.

Then, nearer still, it was obvious how flustered she looked. The pressures of the manic day in ER were clearly getting to her. And just before she reached them, his heart hit the floor. It was equally obvious how unhappy she was.

He saw her hesitate just before she reached them, noticed her swallow hard, and then, as they stood up in anticipation, she gave them the news.

'I'm so sorry to have to tell you...'

Celia's hands went to her face, and she let out a desolate sob.

Daisy wrapped an arm around her, pulled her close as she broke her heart on her shoulder.

The junior nurse dropped her head to the clipboards in her hands, and Aidan said the only thing he could, in a hoarse whisper.

'We're sure you did everything you could, nurse.'

Chapter 38

Aidan had assumed the nurse had dropped her head because of the news she'd had to give them, but that wasn't quite the case.

She fumbled with the paper on the first clipboard, then pulled out the second one, looked at it and shook her head.

'Oh... oh, I'm so sorry. Bit stretched today, you understand? You... you're not the Johnson's, are you?'

'No, we came in with Will... Jack I mean. The guy dressed as a pirate?'

The nurse looked acutely embarrassed. 'I'm so sorry...'

'Yes, you just said that,' growled Daisy curtly.

'Yes, I know. I meant... I'm sorry... for...'

A woman's small, hesitant voice called out from the far side of the waiting room. 'We're the Johnsons...'

'Oh dear,' said the nurse, whose day was getting worse by the minute. 'Please excuse me...'

'Um... what the hell is going on?' said Daisy, as the nurse began to head for the Johnsons, to give them the tragic news instead.

'I'm so sorry... I got the wrong...'

'What about Will?' screamed Celia.

'The pirate? Oh, he's out of surgery. It was successful. He's sleeping off the anaesthetic now. I'm sorry, I got the wrong...'

Celia looked like she was about to start a swordfight all over again. *'Are you telling me we don't look like we're here with a pirate?'*

'As I said, I'm so sorry for the... I have to go.'

She scuttled away to the Johnsons. Daisy wrapped her arms around her daughter, still distraught, but this time for a different reason. 'Ok, dear. It was a genuine mistake. Will has come through, and perhaps we should be grateful, but feel sadness for those other people?'

Celia nodded, and slumped down to the seat, suddenly exhausted. Aidan watched for the acutely-embarrassed nurse to leave the tearful Johnsons to their grief, and stopped her for a quick word.

'Can we see Jack, please?'

'Oh... he's in a critical-care ward now, but he's totally out of it. It'll be at least a couple of hours before he comes round.'

Celia stood up, walked over. 'I don't care. I want to be with him.'

'Well, I'll see what the consultant says. I'm sorry, I have to go.'

'If she apologises one more time, I'll thump her...' growled Celia.

Daisy appeared beside them, a smile finally on her face. 'Leave it be, dear. They're pushed to capacity right now. Let's just be relieved, and see what we can do about making it all better.'

Celia sat quietly by Will's bed, her gaze fixed on him and the wires and pipes connected to various bits of his body. It would still be a while until he woke, but somehow it didn't matter how long it was.

When the man who almost gave his life to save hers opened his eyes, she would be the first thing he saw.

Apart from him, she was alone in the small room. He'd been moved there a half-hour ago, after her parents had pledged to pay whatever was needed for him to have his own private room, for however long it was until he was discharged from Addenbrookes.

211

They'd left a short while ago, to find a train to take them home. Celia had declined to leave with them. She wasn't going anywhere until she knew Will was awake, and truly out of danger.

She was tired; very tired. The time had crept to five in the afternoon, and through the window overlooking the green fields on the other side of the hospital complex, the sun was heading for the horizon, preparing to say goodbye to the day that once again might have just changed her life.

All was at peace. The beeping of the monitors was regular and soothing, and from what little she knew of VSM's, his signs all looked normal. Everything seemed promising, but until he woke from the anaesthetic and spoke encouraging words, the dull ache of dread would still be there, somewhere in the back of her stomach.

A couple of hours ago, a nurse had told her they'd managed to contact his parents. They were on holiday, cruising the Greek islands. They were flying back, and would be there in the next few hours.

Celia settled back, content to wait it out for as long as it took.

She felt sleep trying to take her away, gave herself a mental slap to scare it off. Falling asleep wasn't an option. She grabbed herself a cup of water from the basin in the corner of the room, held its coolness against her brow for a moment, to try to lower her anxiety and make sure sleep knew it wasn't welcome.

She'd only been seated again for two minutes when she heard something. The constant regular beeping from the VSM had masked it, but somehow she knew she'd heard it.

Then it was there again. A quiet murmur. Will's head moved, just a fraction, and she saw the bedclothes rise as he sucked in a deeper breath.

He was coming round.

Chapter 39

His eyelids slowly parted. For a moment his eyes looked blank, and then they moved a little to the left, and then the right.

Celia drew her chair as close to the bed as it would go, called his name softly. 'Will, are you in there somewhere?'

His eyes focussed on her face, a thousand questions spearing into her. Then a slight smile broke across his face. 'Elizabeth.'

'Will.'

'Where... where am I?'

'Addenbrookes. Will, you almost died.'

His head lay back on the pillow. 'What are you doing here?'

'*Really?* You were almost killed saving my life, and you ask why I'm here?'

He smiled. 'I do feel like I've just eaten a killer vindaloo. I don't remember what happened, after the sword...'

'That thug Sergei ran you through, after you deliberately put yourself in front of me. You fell unconscious, until now.'

'Wow. I really should be dead.'

'Yes, you should. The consultant said the sword had severed your lower intestine. They went in through the same incision and sewed everything back up again, so you'll only have a swordblade-sized scar.'

'Right now I don't think I care. It's just good to be still alive. So what happened after I fell asleep?'

'I... kinda lost it. I slashed at Sergei for what he'd done, so crazily he stepped back, right onto my mother's sword.'

'Is he here too?'

'No. He died at the scene.'

'Guess I *was* the lucky one then.'

'Lucky? You almost lost your life to save me. What's lucky about that?'

'I said I would protect you, Elizabeth.'

She lowered her eyes. 'The pirate adventure is over... Jack. I might still be wearing the dress, but maybe it's time to start using our real names?'

He shook his head. 'I'm not sure I want it to be over, Celia. I quite enjoyed the fantasy... well, some of it anyway. Real life will see you going home, and us never meeting again.'

'Will it?' She took his hand gently. 'If you want to know, Jack, I enjoyed the fantasy too. Enough to wish it was real life.'

He glanced to the sun setting over the fields. 'Is that why you're still here, because I must have been out of it a really long time.'

She let out a nervous laugh. 'You know what pirates say... you saved my life, so I belong to you now.'

'I'm not into possessions, Celia.'

'Neither am I. But apparently I saved your life too way back, so perhaps we really do belong to each other.'

He took his hand away from hers. 'That's all fantasy. The real truth is I'm a penniless actor, who leapt at the opportunity to play a fantasy role on a fantasy ship, and then succumbed to the temptation of a rich reward if I mutinied. So rather like fantasy, we're totally different people, and I'm not the man you think I am.'

His words made her angry. 'So the fact you risked your life to save mine is just fantasy too then?'

'Well... no, perhaps not. But I'm still not worthy of someone like you.'

215

'*Someone like me?* I bared my soul to you on the quarterdeck that night, Jack. But then after I realised you were a part of the mutiny, if there'd been hard drugs within reach I would have turned right back there. So what kind of a *lady* does that make me?'

He shook his head. 'That makes it even worse, don't you see? Because of my stupid decisions you almost went back to your demons. And that makes me bad news, doesn't it?'

She took a sip of water, to help calm her fraught emotions. 'That's not the way to see it, Jack. I'm walking on the top of a narrow wall right now, and I could fall either way. But that night it was my decision to want to find comfort in what was familiar to me. I couldn't find that comfort, luckily. But...'

'But?'

'Don't you see? When we kissed...'

'Actually, it was you who kissed me...'

'That's irrelevant,' she snapped. 'When we kissed, it did something inside me. I didn't go back to my cabin and want to find drugs just because I felt happy. I didn't *need* to. You gave me something beautiful, and I didn't even think about awful substances. It was only when I believed you'd joined the long line of men who'd betrayed me...'

'I see your point. But it doesn't make any relevant difference. I'm a poor out-of-work actor, living in a basement apartment in Mundesley. I literally have nothing to offer you.'

'Mundesley? I live near Kings Lynn... well, I do now. That's not far away at all.'

He reached out for her hand. 'Celia, listen to me. We could live next door, it wouldn't make any difference. We're from a different class structure. Look at what you're wearing. Daisy and Aidan are obviously well-off, and they'll

216

want something better for you than anything I can offer... especially now you're getting back on your feet.'

Celia stood up, angry at what was undoubtedly one version of the truth. *'What I'm wearing?'* she cried. 'So if the clothes maketh the woman...'

She reached behind her back, unzipped the dress and let it fall to the floor. Standing there in just her bra and panties, she glared at him. *'So now what do you maketh of the woman?'*

A smile broke across his face, but there wasn't time to say anything. The door opened, and a senior staff nurse stood there, a little taken-aback, to say the least.

Celia tried to cover up a few bits of herself she didn't have enough hands for, and grinned inanely at the middle-aged woman. 'Um... that... that dress is really uncomfortable. I just needed to take it off for a while...'

The nurse tut-tutted her disapproval. 'I think I can find you a hospital gown, if you'd like, miss?' she said stiffly.

'Oh... yes please.'

She walked over to Jack, took his pulse and studied the VSM. 'Glad to see you are awake, Jack. I must fetch the consultant to check you over properly.'

With a sideways glance at Celia, she was gone. She and Jack laughed out the amusement they were trying to hold in for matron's sake, until Jack grabbed his stomach. *'Oww...* don't make me laugh. It hurts too much.'

'Oh hell, I'm so sorry.' Celia passed him a cup of water, fed him a sip. 'So *do* you see me differently now?'

He smiled, looked her almost nakedness up and down. 'Not really. You're still totally gorgeous.'

She lowered her eyes. 'You know what I mean.'

'Well...'

He didn't get any further. The door opened again, and the consultant walked in, a nurse in tow with a gown over her arm. She handed it to a grateful but sheepish Celia, and she slipped it on as the consultant poked and prodded Jack.

After a couple of minutes he smiled, threw a quick glance to the now covered-up Celia. 'You seem to be doing well, young man. But I must advise you against any... excitement right now. The nurse will come later to change your dressings.'

They left together, and it was just the two of them again. Jack laid his head back on the pillow, and then laid the facts on the line for Celia. 'I don't have a single piece of eight, Celia. It's truly awesome and humbling you've been here all this time for me, but it doesn't alter the fact I have nothing to offer you. Not now, and not in the future.'

'Hang on... your parents are cruising the Greek islands. That's hardly a cheap holiday, so don't give me the penniless crap.'

He looked up, startled. 'How do you know that?'

'The staff told me. They managed to reach them, and they're flying back. They should be here soon.'

He didn't look too pleased. 'I'm surprised they're bothering.'

'Jack?'

'Look... if you must know they're quite rich. My father disowned me a few years ago. We've had hardly any contact since then. He's a legal eagle, pretty high up the law chain. Bit of a dinosaur in some ways.'

'Ah, I see. So in his world, a son follows his father's footsteps. I take it you didn't?'

'I did, for two years. Studied law at the UEA. But it wasn't for me, the lure of treading the boards too great. So I dropped out. He was disgusted.'

'That stinks. But we do have something in common after all. I studied law too, here in Cambridge, until my so-called boyfriend got me into drugs so he could have his wicked way with me. I managed to get through to my finals, but was already on the downward spiral. I failed them, dismally.'

'But your parents didn't disown you, did they?'

'No, maybe because it wasn't my choice to fail. When I went back home I was already a lost cause, but they're not the type to throw in the towel on hopeless cases. They tried to help, but then I got taken. I disappeared off the face of the Earth, but they still didn't give up.'

'Wow. Go them.'

'But the first point is, I was in Uganda, and had no idea they *hadn't* given up on me. Maybe your parents haven't given up on you, you just don't know it. They're coming here, aren't they?'

He nodded. 'Yes, out of a misplaced sense of parental duty, maybe.'

'Perhaps. Perhaps not.'

'You said *first point*, like there are more?'

'Just one that I can think of right now. But it's a very important one. In a weird kind of way, we're both lost causes. We both succumbed to different temptations, and now regret it. But I don't intend to be a lost cause any longer. What about you, Jack? Are you going to be a waste of space for the rest of your life?'

He looked away, a strange expression on his face, half-smiling, half agonised. 'I guess you're not going to let me, are you?'

'Absolutely not.'

The door that didn't seem to want to stay closed opened again, and a smartly-dressed man and woman walked into the room. '*Jack...*' his mother cried.

Celia grabbed the beautiful dress that was looking a little less beautiful than it once did, gave Jack a kiss on the cheek, and headed for the door. She threw a disdainful look at his parents as she passed them by.

'I'll leave you to be with him now. And I doubt he'll tell you, so I will. Your brave son almost gave his life to save mine. I think that makes him a hero, doesn't it?'

Chapter 40

Five days later, Daisy and Aidan sat together in DCI Burrow's office, feeling a little like schoolchildren brought up in front of the headmaster.

At one end of the desk, Sarah sat in a third chair, feeling exactly the same. The headmaster sat at his desk, black-rimmed glasses hanging off his nose, thumbing through pages of statements that he'd spread out across the top, in an effort to make sense of the words.

No one had said a single sentence for a few minutes, but then Burrows cleared his throat and looked up. 'You do realise the Norfolk Chief of Police wants an explanation as to why two of his officers were directly involved in an incident that took place in a different county, don't you? And none of these statements are exactly helping my case.'

'I'm so sorry, Inspector,' said Daisy quietly.

'Are you? Then why do your words sound more like fantasy than reality?'

Aidan smiled mirthlessly. 'Perhaps because what we went through was exactly that.'

Burrows went back to thumbing through the sheets of paper. 'Old curses? Ghosts of voodoo sorceresses? People getting hung from the yardarm? I'm starting to think I'm about to be posted to Port Royal.'

'Actually, there's not much of it left above the sea level these days,' Daisy offered.

'Is that supposed to be funny?'

'No, sir,' Daisy lowered her eyes, suitably chastised.

'Actually, sir, it was your decision to drive us to Essex. And if you hadn't, I shudder to think what would have happened,' Sarah reminded her boss.

'Wasn't there enough that happened anyway? Two deaths, one almost-death?'

'Jack is doing well, thank you for asking, Inspector,' Daisy said pointedly.

Burrows sighed. 'I suppose that yet again, I have to give you the benefit of the doubt, Daisy Morrow.'

'Yes, Inspector, I think you do.'

Sarah defended her friends. 'We were all there, sir. Sergei Romanov definitely backed swiftly into Daisy sword. She couldn't have avoided killing him.'

'Hmm... right sword, wrong time, hey Daisy?'

'You want the truth, Inspector? It was totally accidental. It all happened so quickly, I couldn't have moved my sword out of the way, even if I'd wanted to. But I'll tell you now, and it doesn't go any further than these four walls, ok?' Burrows nodded in a resigned kind of way. 'If I had had time to move it out of the way, I can't be sure if I would have bothered or not.'

Burrows shook his head. 'So should I charge you with possession of a lethal weapon then, Daisy?'

'That's your right, Inspector.'

'Sir...' Sarah pleaded.

'It's ok, Lowry. I'm not going to. That... lethal weapon is state's evidence now, and won't ever see the light of day again.'

'Inspector, that cost a fortune...' Daisy begged, until Burrows gave her a stare over the top of his spectacles. 'Sorry,' she said quietly, and went back to twiddling her thumbs.

Aidan asked a question. 'I don't suppose the police are any nearer knowing who killed Barbossa... sorry, Ilya Komanichov?

Burrows shook his head. 'Somehow I don't think we ever will be. The divers recovered his body two days ago, which as you know had been submerged in the engine room, sat under water for three days before we got to it. Any evidence there might have been was lost to the sea.'

'A bit like Barbossa,' said Daisy.

'Daisy...'

'Sorry.'

Burrows started to shuffle the papers together. 'I suppose these statements will have to do. Once more you seem to have got away with... dubious exploits, Daisy.'

'We did help you apprehend a dangerous Russian criminal, Inspector. Can I ask what is likely to happen to him?'

Burrows sighed. 'We're going to charge him with Ilya Komanichov's murder, but it's highly unlikely to stick.'

'Then why bother?' said Aidan.

'To add weight to the other charges we're bringing. Endangering human life, the taking of hostages, attempted theft of a valuable item, twice, and a few other things. He'll be going away for a number of years, trust me.'

'Then it's a result,' smiled Daisy. 'May we go now?'

'Just one more thing,' Burrows said, sounding exactly like Columbo. 'There is one glaring inaccuracy in these statements.'

'Really?' said Daisy.

'Oh yes... this nonsense about Tia Dalma being a ghost.'

'It's not nonsense, Inspector. It's really the only explanation,' said Aidan.

'Please.'

'It's true. How else do you explain how she came and went? She wasn't on the guest list, wasn't in the lifeboats or rescued from the ship... she wasn't anywhere.'

'I... I can't explain that. But I can assure you she wasn't a ghost.'

'So how can you be so sure?'

He fumbled through the papers, pulled out a photocopy that had been hidden by the statements. 'Because MI6 faxed me this an hour ago. It was published in the Moscow State Newspaper yesterday. That's the original photo, but they translated the Russian for us...'

Daisy's eyes opened wide as she looked at the picture of the Crimson Heart, hung around the neck of a black bust which was encased in a glass display box.

The headline took her breath away...

CRIMSON HEART BACK WHERE IT BELONGS

And underneath the photo, just a few words of explanation...

Mystery surrounds an incident at the Moscow State Museum whichtook place last night. On arriving for work this morning, the curatorswere astonished to find the precious pendant back in its display case, after it had been stolen three months ago.
No explanation has been given for this strange occurrence, but the chief curator said this morning, "We are all so happy the Crimson Heart has been returned to its rightful place".

Aidan was grinning from ear to ear. 'So the one Tia dropped over the side was another fake. Go her!'

'Didn't see that coming either,' said a slightly-disgruntled Daisy.

Burrows shook his head. 'So, perhaps you three would like to modify your statements now, and remove the word *ghost*?'

Daisy and Aidan shook Burrows' hand, and headed for the door. Just before they left, Daisy thought of something else she needed to ask. 'Inspector, what happens to Jack now?'

'Who?' he grinned.

'You know, the mutineer who saved our daughter's life?'

He waved a hand dismissively in the air. 'Oh, you mean the ghost... guest. Bit hard to make any charges stick to an apparition, don't you think?'

Daisy and Aidan sat at a small table outside the Kings Lynn docks cafe, sipping lattes before heading home to Great Wiltingham.

'Our dear Inspector will have a little grovelling to do to his chief,' Aidan mused.

'I suppose so. But he's a good old stick deep down, so I'm sure he'll be fine.'

'So Tia Dalma wasn't a ghost after all. She just moves in mysterious ways,' Aidan said, and then noticed his wife wasn't looking too happy. 'Considering all is relatively well, dear, you don't look particularly enamoured with life?'

'I guess I'm not. It's really ticking me off.'

'What is?'

'We didn't solve the mystery this time. Dimitri Novalenko swears it wasn't him, and quite honestly I can't believe doing away with Ilya would serve any of his criminal purposes. So we don't know who killed Barbossa.'

Aidan grinned cheekily. 'Don't we, dear?'

225

Daisy nodded thoughtfully, went back to sipping her coffee, and said no more about it. But then, as they wandered back to the car, someone else was filling her thoughts.

'Celia and Jack seem quite taken with each other, dear. She's still staying at the Cambridge Travelodge so she can be with him while he recovers. I think there may be a blossoming romance there.'

'You could be right, Flower. I'm getting a distinct feeling of déjà vu. We met when you saved my life.'

'Not forgotten, dear. And we turned out alright in the end.'

'*In the end?*' he looked aghast.

'Well, you were clearly smitten with the beautiful blonde agent who swooped in out of nowhere and stole your heart.'

'And you?'

'Well, let's just say I tried my best to pretend you hadn't got under my skin.'

'For how long?'

'Oh, about three days. Then I had to admit you had. *A friggin' accountant...*'

He grinned. 'You are so wicked.'

'Maybe that's why you love me... cos you ain't!'

'Give you that one. I do worry though. Jack is a nice guy, but he's got little in the way of prospects.'

'You still juggling numbers, Dip?'

'I suppose I would just like know Celia is with someone who can take care of her.'

Daisy shook her head as she sank into the passenger seat. 'Taking care of someone isn't just about the numbers, dear. You don't think saving her life is taking care of her? You of all people?'

'Perhaps I should learn from my own experiences,' he smiled, and kissed his wife on the cheek.

'Yes, you should. And also maybe try to understand women better. After all, Jack is so dashing and handsome...'

———

We hope you enjoyed 'Pirates of Great Yarmouth: Curse of the Crimson Heart'. If you could find a minute to leave a review on your favourite site, we would be eternally grateful! It helps others to know what you thought, and gives us feedback too. Thank you!

Look out for the fifth Daisy Morrow adventure...

'The Terrifying Tale of the Homesick Scarecrow'

From feeling like they were back in the eighteenth century, Daisy and Aidan are thrust very much into the twenty-first century.

A call for help turns into a crazy caper even Daisy didn't see coming, as they fight to help stop a dangerous secret from going public.

It's not going to be easy however, because this particular secret has two legs... and a big mouth!

———

228

Here's a Sneaky Preview...

Chapter 1

We've Only Just Begun

'You really don't have to mollycoddle me, dad.'

He grinned as he opened the driver's door. 'I know, but you have to give your mum and me a little licence, Celia. We've not done any mollycoddling for three years, so we've got a little catching up to do.'

She sighed, batting her mother's independent streak to the back of her mind. 'I suppose it's only a ride to the station after all.'

'Exactly. Public transport in Great Wiltingham isn't exactly prolific.'

Daisy chipped in with a smile, as she headed to open the gate. 'And you're still recovering yourself, and now off to look after a wounded soldier.'

Celia followed her mum to the gate. 'I know all that, but don't you think feeling useful is part of the therapy I need?'

Daisy nodded. 'You make a good point, dear. As long as he doesn't end up relying on you too much.'

'Mum... they're only letting him out of Addenbrookes on the basis there's someone at home to look after him.'

Daisy swung the gate open. 'You said his parents asked him to go to their place in Aldburgh. He had a choice.'

'He wanted to be in his own home. They're going to visit often anyway.'

'Can't imagine why he'd rather be with you than his own parents,' Daisy grinned.

'Yes you can.'

'Ok, I can. Just... just remember we're on the end of the phone, ok?'

'You'll probably get sick of me calling.'

'I hope so... oh, you know what I mean.'

Celia gave her mum a hug. 'Of course I do. It's only for a couple of weeks while he gets on his feet.'

'And then?'

'Let's just see, yeah?'

They were just about to turn and head to the car when Daisy caught sight of someone on the pavement outside, shuffling slowly past. He grinned warmly, lifted a hand in greeting.

She smiled back. 'Walter... haven't seen you in ages.'

He stopped shuffling as Daisy went over to him as he opened his arms, the walking stick waving in the air. 'Hello, you old wrinklie. Give us a kiss quick, before Aidan sees.'

She hugged him, gave him a peck on the cheek. 'How have you been, soldier?'

He leant a slightly-shaky hand on the gate. 'Oh, you know how it is. Those pesky jerries don't leave us alone. Every night, wave after wave of them. Just no time to relax. But we got two of them last night.'

Celia was looking curious, so Daisy explained. 'Walter is an ARP warden. He mans one of the searchlights most nights. He's very good at his job too.'

'But...'

He grinned, showing his perfect false teeth. 'It's hard work, defending Norwich from those bastards.'

'But...'

'Don't worry, my dear. They're unlikely to bomb Great Wiltingham,' Walter reassured her.

Daisy tapped her daughter's arm. 'We're safe here, Celia.'

Walter made to leave. 'Well Daisy, must go. Back on duty in two hours. Have to make myself a few ham sandwiches before then. Be safe, my dears.'

He ambled off, shuffling his slow way along the lane with a backwards wave of his hand.

Celia looked at her mum. 'That poor man. He still thinks it's World War Two. How old is he?'

'Ninety-one. But it is still WW2, dear. When he closes his eyes anyway.'

'Mum, you're not making sense. He's not well.'

Daisy grinned. 'Actually, he's the wellest person I know. And the sanest. Which is not saying a lot, given the village residents.'

'Mum, I know you're a little bit crazy, but...'

'Dear, most of the village thinks he's lost his mind. But he's well aware it's the twenty-first century. Last time we met, we were discussing the pros and cons of Boris Johnson.'

'I think you need to explain.'

'Ok... you know you young people spend a small fortune on computer games and virtual reality headsets to play war games?'

'Well, some of us do.'

'Point taken. So, Walter doesn't need any technology. When he wants to, he just closes his eyes and he's back there. For real. And he goes there pretty much every night.'

'But how? I mean...'

'He got blown up by a doodlebug in nineteen-forty-two. When they put him back together and discharged him, a few weeks later he discovered he could transport himself back there, relive what he sees as his glory days, in glorious Technicolor. He actually *does* go back there, for hours at a time.'

'Wow... if Sony could tap into whatever he does, they'd make a fortune.'

'Actually, that's the last thing they'd want to do. Think about it... no console, no VR headsets or CD games... what would they sell?'

Celia grinned. 'Good point. I guess I'll just have to accept strange things go on in this seemingly-innocent village.'

'Well, Walter is the Wiltingham Enigma for sure!'

Daisy gave her daughter a hug, and reminded her she was on the end of the phone any time day or night, and then watched as the car drove away.

She walked slowly back to the kitchen, her mind a mess of contradicting feelings. She'd only had a couple of weeks since the Black Pearl incident to spend time with her daughter, before Celia had announced Jack was being discharged and she was going to Mundesley to care for him while he recovered the strength to look after himself.

Daisy couldn't argue, although she would have liked to have found something to argue with. The guy did save her daughter's life, and if he hadn't been so brave, Celia wouldn't have been around at all.

It was the only thing she could do now, and they all knew it.

So once again she was gone, but at least this time only on the end of a phone. She smiled to herself at what Celia had said. Feeling needed and wanted would be good for her. There was no doubt about that.

But in a few days, a quick visit to the North Norfolk coast might be a nice day out for the parents.

The parents settled down quite early that night, after Aidan had confiscated Daisy's phone as the only way to stop her calling Celia.

She'd let out a few frustrated expletives, but knew he was right. Their daughter was twenty-five after all, and quite old and intelligent enough to make her own decisions.

But as Daisy pointed out as she switched off the bedside table lamp, she *was* her mother.

Celia had called a few hours ago, to let them know Jack was home, and all was well. But Daisy's mumsy instincts were still making their presence felt, and sleep was a while coming, until finally it took her away... for about two hours.

She woke suddenly, but the reason was obvious straightaway. Aidan's phone was going off on his bedside table, and he was reaching out to answer it. Instantly, Daisy felt the pang of fear thump into her stomach.

'*Celia?*' she whispered, as Aidan shook his head and answered the phone, switching it to speaker.

'Charlie?'

His brother sounded frantic. '*Ade, I'm so sorry to ring you at this hour. I didn't know who else to ring... can't trust anyone...*'

'Charlie, calm down. What's happened?'

'*Oh Christ... the worst thing ever... it's a nightmare, and only just beginning...*'

'Charlie, you're not making sense. Tell me what's wrong.'

'*Oh hell. Not over the phone. I know it's three in the morning, but can you guys come. Please?*'

Aidan glanced to Daisy. She nodded her head, slipping out of bed and grabbing a few clothes at the same time.

233

'We'll be there in thirty, Charlie. Just keep calm. Grab a drink or something.'

'Thanks.'

'What on Earth could have happened?' said Daisy nervously as they set off in the car.

'Your guess is as good as mine. He said he couldn't trust anyone. But the farm is only fifteen miles away, so we'll soon find out.'

'I thought he was retired now? He's been reclusive for the last four years, ever since…'

'I know. We've tried to bring him out of it, and failed dismally, dear. How many times did we ask him to join us for dinner at the pub in Cawston?'

'About fifteen. He always said he was too busy, whatever that meant for a reclusive retiree.'

'Now I'm starting to wonder if he did actually retire. A brain like his always needs something to do.'

'And he doesn't have me to occupy his mind like you do, dear.'

As they drove into the old farm that wasn't a farm anymore, nothing seemed out of place. But as a fraught Charlie met them at the farmhouse door, he looked anything but in place.

'Thank God. I'm so sorry, you two…'

'It's fine, Charlie. We've not had an adventure for at least two weeks,' said Daisy, only slightly sarcastically.

Aidan frowned to her to button it. 'Charlie, you'd better tell us what's happened.'

He poured them a couple of brandies, sank the remains of his in one gulp. 'Trust me, I guarantee you've never had an adventure like this before…'

'Just tell us, please?'

'You'd better sit down. It's a long and extremely embarrassing story.'

Daisy and Aidan did as he said at the kitchen table. 'We're all ears.'

Charlie was still pacing the flagstone floor, empty glass in hand. Aidan said firmly. 'Charlie, come and sit down, and start at the beginning.'

He pulled out a chair. Aidan handed him a fresh brandy, and as his head lowered, he began to tell them why he was in such a state.

'First off, I've not been honest with you... well, not with anyone. I couldn't, it was just too big.'

'What was?'

'I didn't retire, not totally. I'd been working on something four years ago, before... before it happened. When I lost my appetite to work on contracts for MI6 anymore, I came here to shut myself away, but didn't stop... pushing the boundaries of technology.'

'That's what you did so well, Charlie... creating the genius gadgets MI6 agents use, as a private contractor.'

'It *was* what I did well. But when I came here, I took things a step further, invented the biggest... gadget of all.'

'So this farm is just a front?'

'Partly. I did buy it because I wanted to be alone. But then I lost myself in work, and made a breakthrough. A *massive* breakthrough.' He shuddered, like it was hard to even talk about.

'Hey, Charlie.' Daisy reached out a hand, wrapped it around his shaking forearm. 'So no one knew about this?'

'Just Rupert. He gave me a covert green light to work in secret. No one else knew.'

235

'Rupert has just retired himself. He helped me out a few months ago, just before he was about to leave MI6.'

'When he retired, we agreed he couldn't tell anyone at SIS about... about this. The potential was just too big. Apart from you two, he's the only other person who knows... knows he exists. At least, I thought he was.'

'He?'

Charlie shook his head. 'You'd better refill your glasses, folks. The story I'm about to tell you will blow your socks off. It all began two days ago...'

————

Read all about the Daisy Morrow series at
rtgreen.net/daisy-morrow

COME AND JOIN US!

We'd love you to become a VIP Reader.

Our intro library is the most generous in publishing!
Join our mail list and grab it all for free.
We really do appreciate every single one of you,
so there's always a freebie or two coming along,
news and updates, advance reads of new releases...

Head here to get started...
rtgreen.net

Printed in Great Britain
by Amazon